Broken April

A Note on Pronunciation

The Albanian alphabet is phonetic; it sometimes uses two letters to indicate a single sound. Some Albanian letters have sound values that do not coincide with those of English. Among them are the following letters, which occur in proper names in *Broken April*:

Vowels

ë	an unstressed vowel, like "a" in "a lot"
y	German "u" or the "u" of French "rendu, attendu," etc.

Consonants

c	"ts" as in "curtsy"
ç	"ch" as in "church"
dh	voiced "th" as in "there"
gj	"g" as in "gem"
j	"y" as in "yellow"
q	a sound approximating the shortened sound of "tu" as in "future"

BROKEN APRIL

Ismail Kadare, born in 1936 in the Albanian mountain town of Girokaster near the Greek border, studied in Tirana and at the Gorky institute, Moscow. He is Albania's best-known poet and novelist. His works have been translated worldwide. He established an uneasy modus vivendi with the Communist authorities until their attempts to turn his reputation to their advantage drove him, in 1990, to seek asylum in France, for, as he says, 'Dictatorship and authentic literature are incompatible...The writer is the natural enemy of dictatorship'. He lives in Paris.

Ismail Kadare

BROKEN APRIL

TRANSLATED FROM THE ALBANIAN

VINTAGE

Published by Vintage 2003

2 4 6 8 10 9 7 5 3 1

Copyright © Librairie Arthème Fayard 1982
Translation copyright © New Amsterdam Books
and Saqi Books 1990

Ismail Kadare has asserted his right under the Copyright,
Designs and Patents Act, 1988 to be identified as the author
of this work

First published in Great Britain in 1990 by
Saqi Books, London

Vintage
Random House, 20 Vauxhall Bridge Road,
London SW1V 2SA

Random House Australia (Pty) Limited
20 Alfred Street, Milsons Point, Sydney
New South Wales 2061, Australia

Random House New Zealand Limited
18 Poland Road, Glenfield,
Auckland 10, New Zealand

Random House (Pty) Limited
Endulini, 5A Jubilee Road, Parktown 2193,
South Africa

The Random House Group Limited Reg. No. 954009
www.randomhouse.co.uk

A CIP catalogue record for this book
is available from the British Library

ISBN 0 099 44987 0

Papers used by Random House are natural, recyclable
products made from wood grown in sustainable forests.
The manufacturing processes conform to the environ-
mental regulations of the country of origin

Printed and bound in Denmark by
Nørhaven Paperback, Viborg

CHAPTER I

His feet were cold, and each time he moved his numbed legs a little he heard the desolate grating of pebbles under his shoes. But the sense of desolation was really inside him. Never before had he stayed motionless for so long, lying in wait behind a ridge that overlooked the highway.

Daylight was fading. Fearful or simply troubled, he brought the rifle's stock to his cheek. Soon it would be dusk, and he would not be able to see the sights of the weapon in the fading light. "He's sure to come by before it's too dark to take aim," his father had said. "Just be patient and wait."

Slowly the gun barrel swept over some patches of the half-thawed snow towards the wild pomegranates scattered through the brush-covered space on both sides of the road. For perhaps the hundredth time he thought that this was a fateful day in his life. Then the gun barrel swung back again to where it had been. What in his mind he had called a fateful day was no more than those patches of snow and those wild pomegranates that seemed to have been waiting since midday to see what he would do.

He thought, soon night will fall and it will be too dark to shoot. He wished that dusk would come swiftly, that night would race on after it, so that he could run away from this accursed ambush. It was the second time in his life that he had lain in wait to take revenge, but the man he must kill was the same one, so that this ambush was really an extension of the other.

He became aware again of his icy feet, and he moved his legs as if to keep the cold from rising in his body, but it had long since reached his belly, his chest and even his head. He had the feeling that bits of his brain had frozen, like those patches of snow along the sides of the road.

He felt that he could not shape a clear thought. He had only a vague animosity for the wild pomegranates and the patches of snow, and sometimes he told himself that were it not for them, he would have given up his vigil long ago. But there they were, motionless witnesses that had kept him from going away.

At the bend in the road, for perhaps the twentieth time that day, he thought he saw the man he had been waiting for. The man came on with short steps; the black barrel of his rifle rose above his right shoulder. The watcher started. This time it was no hallucination. It really was the man he was waiting for.

Just as he had done so many times before, Gjorg brought the rifle to his shoulder and took aim at the man's head. For a moment the head seemed to resist him, trying to elude his sights, and at the last instant he even thought he saw an ironic smile on the man's face. Six months before, the same thing had happened, and so as not to disfigure that face (who can say whence that touch of pity came at the last moment?) he had lowered the front sight of his weapon and wounded his enemy in the neck.

The man came closer. Please not a wound this time, Gjorg said to himself in a kind of prayer. His family had had great trouble paying the fine for the first wound, and a second fine would ruin them. But there was no penalty for death.

The man came closer. Gjorg thought, better a clean miss than a wound. As he had done each time he had imagined he saw the man, in keeping with the custom, he warned the man before he fired. Neither then nor later did he know if he had called aloud or if the words had been stifled in his throat. In fact the other man turned his head sharply. Gjorg saw him move his arm as if to unsling the rifle from his shoulder, and he fired. Then he raised his head, and as if bewildered watched the dead man—still standing, but Gjorg was sure he had killed him—take a step forward, drop his rifle on the right side, and immediately fall to the left.

Gjorg came out of concealment and walked towards the body. The road was deserted. The only sound was the sound of his own footsteps. The dead man had fallen in a heap. Gjorg bent down and laid his hand on the man's shoulder, as if to wake him. "What am I doing?" he said to himself. He gripped the dead man's shoulder again, as if he wanted to bring him back to life. "Why am I doing this?" he thought. At once he realized that he had bent down over the other man not to awaken him from eternal sleep

9

but to turn him on his back. He simply meant to follow the custom. Around him patches of snow were still there, scattered witnesses.

He stood up and was about to leave when he remembered that he had to put the dead man's rifle near his head.

He did it all as if in a dream. He felt like vomiting, and he told himself several times that it must be because of the blood. A few moments later he was fleeing down the deserted road, almost at a run.

Dusk was falling. He looked back two or three times without knowing why. The road was still completely empty. In the dying day the still deserted road stretched away between brush and thicket.

Somewhere ahead he heard mule bells, then human voices, and he saw a group of people. In the twilight it was hard to tell whether they were visitors or mountain folk returning from the market. They came up with him sooner than he had expected. Men, young women, and children.

They said, "Good evening," and he stopped. Even before he spoke, he motioned in the direction from which he had come. Then he said in a hoarse voice, "Over there by the bend in the road I killed a man. Turn him on his back, good people, and put his rifle by his head."

The little group was still. Then a voice asked, "You're not blood-sick are you?" He did not answer. The voice suggested a remedy, but he did not hear it. He had started walking again. Now that he had asked them to turn over the dead man's body as it should be, he felt relieved. He could not remember whether or not he had done that himself. The *Kanun** provided for a state of shock on the

_____

* The code of customary law.

part of the killer, and permitted passers-by to complete whatever he had not been able to do. In any case, to leave a dead man face-down, his weapon far off, was an unforgivable disgrace.

Night had not yet fallen when he reached the village. It was still his fateful day. The door of the *kulla*** was ajar. He pushed it open with his shoulder and went in.

"Well?" someone asked from inside.

He nodded.

"When?"

"Just now."

He heard footsteps coming down the wooden stairs.

"There's blood on your hands," his father said. "Go and wash them."

"It must have happened when I turned him over."

He had tormented himself needlessly. A glance at his hands would have told him that he had done everything in keeping with the rules.

There was a smell of roasted coffee in the *kulla*. Astonishingly, he was sleepy. He yawned twice. The gleaming eyes of his little sister, who leaned against his left shoulder, seemed far away, like two stars beyond a hill.

"And now?" he said suddenly, to no one in particular.

"We must tell the village about the death," his father answered. Only then did Gjorg notice that his father was putting on his shoes.

He was drinking coffee his mother had made for him when he heard, outside, the first shout:

"Gjorg of the Berisha has shot Zef Kryeqyqe."

The voice, with its peculiar ring, sounded at once like

** A stone dwelling in the form of a tower, peculiar to the mountain regions of Albania.

11

the call of a town crier and the singing of an ancient psalmist.

That inhuman voice roused him from his drowsiness for an instant. He felt as if his name had quitted his body, his chest, his skin, to pour itself cruelly outside. It was the first time he had ever felt anything like that. Gjorg of the Berisha, he repeated within him the cry of the pitiless herald. He was twenty-six, and for the first time his name plumbed the depths of life.

Outside the messengers of death, as if on wings, spread that name everywhere.

Half an hour later, they brought back the man's body. Following the custom, they had put him on a litter made of four beech branches. Some still hoped that he was not dead.

The victim's father waited at the door of his house. When the men bearing his son were forty paces off, he called out:

"What have you brought me? A wound or a death?"

The answer was short, dry.

"A death."

His tongue sought moisture, deep, deep in his mouth. Then he spoke painfully:

"Carry him in and tell the village and our kin of our bereavement."

The bells of the cattle returning to the village of Brezftoht, the bell tolling vespers, and all the other sounds of nightfall seemed laden with news of the death.

The streets and lanes were unusually lively for that evening hour. Torches that looked cold in the waning light flickered somewhere at the edge of the village. People came and went by the house of the dead man and by the

12

house of his murderer, going in and coming out. Others, in twos and threes, went off and came back.

At the windows of houses on the outskirts, people exchanged the latest news:

"Have you heard? Gjorg Berisha has killed Zef Kryeqyqe."

"Gjorg Berisha has taken back his brother's blood."

"Are the Berishas going to ask for the twenty-four hour *bessa*?"*

"Yes, of course."

The windows of the tall stone houses looked upon the comings and goings in the village streets. Now night had fallen. The torchlight seemed to thicken as if solidifying. Little by little it turned a deep red, lava springing from mysterious depths, and sparks flew upward from it as if announcing the bloodletting to come.

Four men, one of them elderly, were walking towards the dead man's house.

"The deputation is going to ask for the twenty-four hour *bessa* for the Berishas," someone said from a window.

"Will they grant it?"

"Yes, of course."

Nevertheless, the entire clan of the Berisha were preparing to defend themselves. Here and there you could hear voices: Murrash, go home at once! Cen, close the door. Where's Prenga?

The doors of all the houses of the clan, of kinsfolk near and distant, were closing, for this was the moment of danger, before the victim's family had granted either of the

---

* The pledged word, faith, truce.

13

two periods of truce; according to the Code, the Krye-qyqe, blinded by the newly shed blood, had the right to take vengeance on any member of the Berisha family.

All watched at their windows to see the delegation come out again. "Will they grant the truce?" the women asked.

At last the four mediators came out. The discussion had been short. Their bearing gave nothing away but a voice soon gave out the news.

"The Kryeqyqe family has granted the *bessa*."

Everyone knew that it was the short truce, the twenty-four hour *bessa*. As for the long *bessa*, the thirty-day truce, no one spoke of it yet, for only the village could ask for it—and in any case it could not be requested until after the burial of the last victim.

The voices flew from house to house:

"The Kryeqyqe family has granted the *bessa*."

"*Bessa* has been granted by the Kryeqyqes."

"And a good thing, too. At least we'll have twenty-four hours without bloodshed," a hoarse voice breathed from behind a shutter.

The funeral took place the next day around noon. The professional mourners came from afar, clawing their faces and tearing their hair according to the custom. The old churchyard was filled with the black tunics of the men who had come to the burial. After the ceremony, the funeral cortege returned to the Kryeqyqes' house. Gjorg, too, walked in the procession. At first he had refused to take part in the ceremony, but at last he had given in to his father's urging. He had said, "You must go to the burial. You must also go to the funeral dinner to honor the man's soul."

14

"But I am the *Gjaks*,"* Gjorg had protested. "I'm the one who killed him. Why must I go?"

"For that very reason you must go," his father declared. "If there is anyone who cannot be excused from the burial and the funeral dinner today, it's you." "But why?" Gjorg had asked one last time. "Why must I go?" But his father glared at him and Gjorg said no more.

Now he walked among the mourners, pale, with unsteady steps, feeling people's glances glide by him and turn aside at once, losing themselves in the banks of mist. Most of them were relatives of the dead man. Perhaps for the hundredth time he groaned inwardly: Why must I be here?

Their eyes showed no hatred. They were cold as the March day, as he himself had been cold, without hatred, yesterday evening as he lay in wait for his quarry. Now the newly dug grave, the crosses of stone and wood—most of them askew—and the plaintive sound of the tolling bell, all these struck home. The faces of the mourners, with the hideous scratches left by their fingernails (God, he thought, how did they get their nails to grow so long in twenty-four hours?), their hair torn out savagely and their eyes swollen, the muffled footsteps all around him, all these trappings of death—it was he who had brought them about. And as if that were not enough, he was forced to walk in that solemn cortege, slowly, in mourning, just like them.

The braid on the seams of their tight trousers of white felt nearly touched his own, like poisonous black snakes ready to strike. But he was calm. He was better protected

---

* From the Albanian *gjak* (blood), killer, but with no pejorative connotation, since the *gjaks* is fulfilling his duty under the provisions of the *Kanun*.

15

by the twenty-four hour truce than by the loophole of any *kulla* or fortress. The barrels of their rifles were aligned straight upwards against their short, black tunics, but for the time being they were not free to shoot at him. Perhaps tomorrow or the day after. And if the village asked for the thirty-day *bessa* on his behalf, he would be at peace for another four weeks. And then. . . .

But a few paces ahead of him a rifle barrel swayed as if to stand out among the others. Another barrel, a short one, was to his left. Still others were all around him. Which of them. . . . at the last moment, in his mind, the words "will kill me" changed—as if to soften them—to "will fire at me."

The road from the graveyard to the dead man's house seemed endless. And he still had before him an even more arduous test, the funeral dinner. He would sit at the table with the dead man's kin. They would pass the bread to him, they would set food before him, spoons, forks, and he would have to eat.

Two or three times he felt the urge to get out of that absurd situation, to bolt from the funeral cortege. Let them insult him, jeer at him, accuse him of violating age-old custom, let them shoot at his retreating back if they liked, anything so long as he got away from there. But he knew very well that he could never run away, no more than his grandfather, his great-grandfather, his great-great-grandfather, and all his ancestors five hundred, a thousand years before him had been able to run away.

They were coming close to the house of the dead man. The narrow windows above the arch of the house door had been hung with black cloth. Oh, where am I going, he moaned to himself, and while the low door of the *kulla* was still a hundred paces off, he lowered his head so as not to strike against the stone arch.

The funeral meal took place in accordance with the rules. As long as it went on Gjorg thought about his own funeral feast. Which of these people would go there, just as he had come here today, just as his father and his grandfather and his great-grandfather and all his ancestors had gone to such feasts down through the centuries?

The faces of the mourners were still gouged and bloody. Custom forbade them to wash either in the village where the killing had taken place or on the way back. They could wash only after they reached their homes.

The streaks on their faces and foreheads made them look as if they were wearing masks. Gjorg imagined how his own mourners would look when they had gouged their faces. He felt that from now on the lives of all the generations to come in the two families would be an endless funeral feast, each side playing host in turn. And each side, before leaving for the feast, would don that blood-stained mask.

That afternoon, after the funeral meal, there were once again unusual comings and goings in the village. In a few hours, Gjorg Berisha's one-day truce would be at an end, and now the village elders, as the rules required, were preparing to visit the Kryeqyqes to ask for the thirty-day truce, the long *bessa*, in the name of the village.

On the doorsteps of the *kullas*, on the first floors where the women lived, and in the village squares, people talked of nothing else. This was the first blood-taking of that spring, and of course there was much discussion of everything connected with it. The killing had been performed in

17

accordance with the rules, and as for the burial, the funeral feast, the one-day *bessa*, and everything else, these had been carried out with scrupulous obedience to the ancient Code. So the thirty-day truce that the elders were preparing to ask of the Kryeqyqes would certainly be granted.

As people talked and waited for the latest news about the long *bessa*, they recalled the times, recent or long past, when the rules of the Code had been violated in their village and the surrounding region, and even in far places of the endless plateau. They remembered the violators of the Code as well as the harsh penalties exacted. They remembered persons punished by their own families, whole families punished by the village, or even whole villages punished by a group of villages, or by the Banner.* But, luckily, they said with a sigh of relief, no such disgrace had fallen on their village for a long time. Everything had been done according to the old rules, and not for ages had anyone had the insane notion to break them. This latest blood-taking, too, had been done according to the Code, and Gjorg Berisha, the *gjaks*, young though he was, had behaved well at his enemy's burial and at the funeral dinner. The Kryeqyqes would certainly grant him the thirty-day truce. Especially since the village, having requested this kind of truce, could revoke it if the *gjaks* took it into his head to abuse his temporary respite and roam around the countryside boasting of his deed. But no, Gjorg Berisha was not that sort. On the contrary, he had always been thought quiet and sensible, quite the last young fellow one would expect to play the fool.

---

* Literally a flag. By extension, a collection of various villages under the authority of a local chief who was himself the flag-bearer.

The Kryeqyqes granted the long truce late in the afternoon, a few hours before the short one was due to run out.
One of the village elders came to the Berishas to tell them
of the pledge, with renewed advice that Gjorg must not
abuse it, etc.

After the envoy left, Gjorg sat numbly in a corner of the
stone house. He could look forward to thirty days of
safety. After that, death would lurk all around him. He
would go about only in the dark like a bat, hiding from the
sun, the moonlight, and the flicker of torches.

Thirty days, he said to himself. The shot fired from that
ridge above the highway had cut his life in two: the twenty-six years he had lived thus far, and the thirty days that
began on that very day, the seventeenth of March, and
would end on the seventeenth of April. Then the life of a
bat, but he was not counting that any longer.

Out of the corner of his eye, Gjorg looked at the scrap of
landscape visible through the narrow window. Outside it
was March, half-smiling, half-frozen, with the dangerous
mountain light that belonged to March alone. Then April
would come, or rather just the first half of it. Gjorg felt an
emptiness in the left side of his chest. From now on, April
would be tinged with a bluish pain. . . . Yes, that was how
April had always seemed to him—a month with something incomplete about it. April love, as the songs said.
His own unfinished April. Despite everything, it was better this way, he thought, though he could not say what
was better, that he had avenged his brother or that he had
shed blood in this season. It was only half an hour since he
had been granted the thirty-day truce, and already he was
almost used to the idea that his life had been cleft in two.
Now it even seemed to him that it had always been split
like that: one fragment twenty-six years long, slow to the

point of boredom, twenty-six months of March and twenty-six months of April and as many winters and summers; and the other was short, four weeks, impetuous, fierce as an avalanche, half a March and half an April, like two broken branches glittering with frost.

What would he do in the thirty days left to him? During the long *bessa*, people usually hurried to finish what they had not managed to do so far in their lives. If there was no important thing left undone they busied themselves with the tasks of daily life. If it was seed-time, they hastened to sow. If it was harvest-time, they gathered in the sheaves. If it was neither seed-time nor harvest-time, they did even more ordinary things, like fixing the roof. And if that was not necessary, they just wandered about the countryside to see the cranes flying again, or the first October frosts. Generally, engaged men married during this time, but Gjorg would not marry. The young girl to whom he had been engaged, who lived in a distant Banner and whom he had never seen, had died a year ago after a long illness, and since that time there had been no woman in his life.

Without taking his eyes off the bit of misty landscape, he thought of what he might do in the thirty days left to him. At first it seemed a brief time, too brief, a handful of days too few for anything. But a few minutes later this same respite seemed horribly long and absolutely useless.

March seventeenth, he murmured. March twenty-first. April fourth. April eleventh. April seventeenth. Eighteenth. Aprildeath. Then on and on forever, Aprildeath, Aprildeath, and no more May. Never again.

He was mumbling dates in March and April, over and over, when he heard his father's steps coming down from the floor above. He was holding an oilcloth purse.

"Here, Gjorg, it's the five hundred *groschen* for the blood," he said, holding out the purse to him.

Gjorg's eyes opened wide, and he hid his hands behind his back as if to keep them as far as possible from that loathsome purse.

"What?" he said in a faint voice. "Why?"

His father looked at him amazed.

"What? Why? Have you forgotten that the blood tax must be paid?"

"Oh, yes," Gjorg said, relieved.

The purse was still being held out to him, and he reached out his hands.

"The day after tomorrow you'll have to start off for the *Kulla* of Orosh," his father went on. "It's one day's journey on foot."

Gjorg did not want to go anywhere.

"Can't it wait, father? Does the money have to be paid right away?"

"Yes, son, right away. It has to be settled as soon as possible. The blood tax must be paid right after the killing."

The purse was now in Gjorg's right hand. It seemed heavy. In it was all the money the family had saved, scrimping from week to week and month to month in anticipation of just this day.

"The day after tomorrow," his father said again, "to the *Kulla* of Orosh."

He had gone to the window and was looking fixedly at something outside. There was a gleam of satisfaction in his eye.

"Come here," he said to his son, quietly.

Gjorg went to his father.

Outside in the yard a shirt hung on the wire clothesline.

"Your brother's shirt," he said, almost in a whisper. "Mehill's shirt."

Gjorg could not take his eyes from it. It fluttered white in the wind, waving, billowing joyously.

A year and a half after the day that his brother had been killed, his mother had finally washed the shirt he had worn that day. For a year and a half it had hung blood-soaked from the upper storey of the house, as the *Kanun* required, until the blood had been avenged. When bloodstains began to yellow, people said, it was a sure sign that the dead man was in torment, yearning for revenge. The shirt, an infallible barometer, indicated the time for vengeance. By means of the shirt the dead man sent his signals from the depths of the earth where he lay.

How many times, when he was alone, had Gjorg climbed to that fateful upper storey to look at the shirt! The blood turned more and more yellow. That meant that the dead man had found no rest. How many times had Gjorg seen that shirt in his dreams, washed in water and soapsuds, its whiteness shimmering like the spring sky! But in the morning when he awoke it would be there still, spattered with the brown stains of dried blood.

Now at last the shirt was hanging on the clothesline. But strangely it gave Gjorg no comfort.

Meanwhile, like a new banner hoisted after the old one had been hauled down, on the upper storey of the Kryeqyqe *kulla*, they had hung out the bloody shirt of the new victim.

The seasons, hot or cold, would affect the color of the dried blood, and so would the kind of cloth that the shirt was made of, but no one wanted to take such things into account; all those changes would be taken as mysterious messages, whose import no one dared question.

CHAPTER II

Gjorg had been travelling across the High Plateau for several hours, and there was still no sign that the Kulla of Orosh was near.

Under the fine rain, nameless waste lands, or moorlands with names unknown to him, came into view one after another, naked and dreary. Beyond them, he could just make out the line of mountains veiled in mist, and through the veil he thought he saw the pale reflection, multiplied as if in a mirage, of a single great mountain rather than a range of real peaks differing in height. The fog had made them unsubstantial, but it was strange how much more oppressive they seemed than in fine weather, when their rocks and sheer cliffs were plain to see.

Gjorg heard the dull grating of the pebbles under foot. The villages along the road were far apart, and places with administrative functions or with an inn were rarer still.

But had there been more of these, Gjorg would not have stopped in any of them. He had to be at the *Kulla* of Orosh by nightfall, or at worst late in the evening, so that he could return to his own village the next day.

For the most part, the road was nearly deserted. Now and then solitary mountaineers appeared in the fog, headed somewhere, like himself. At a distance, like everything else on that day of mists, they looked anonymous and unsubstantial.

The settlements were as silent as the road. Here and there were a few scattered houses, each with a wavering plume of smoke rising above its steep roof. "A house is a stone building, or hut, or any other structure that has a hearthstone and emits smoke." He did not know why that definition of a dwelling, which appears in the *Kanun* and which he had known since childhood, had come to mind. "No one enters a house without calling out from the courtyard." But I don't mean to knock or go in anywhere, he said to himself plaintively.

The rain was still falling. Along the way he overtook another group of mountaineers, walking in single file, burdened with sacks of corn. Under the load, their backs seemed more stooped than one would expect. He thought, wet grain is heavier. He remembered having carried a sack of corn once in the rain from the storehouse at the subprefecture all the way to his village.

The laden mountaineers fell back behind him, and again he was alone on the highroad. Its edges on either side were sometimes quite clear and sometimes indistinct. In some stretches flooding and landslides had narrowed the roadway. "A road shall be as wide as a flagstaff is long," he said to himself again, and he realized that for some time the *Kanun*'s prescriptions about roads had been running involuntarily through his head. "A road is for the use of men and livestock, for the passage of the living and the passage of the dead."

He smiled. Whatever he did, he could not escape its definitions. It was no use deceiving himself. The *Kanun* was stronger than it seemed. Its power reached everywhere, covering lands, the boundaries of fields. It made its way into the foundations of houses, into tombs, to churches, to roads, to markets, to weddings. It climbed up to mountain pastures, and even higher still, to the very skies, whence it fell in the form of rain to fill the watercourses, which were the cause of a good third of all murders.

When for the first time he had convinced himself that he had to kill a man, Gjorg had called to mind all that part of the Code that dealt with the rules of the blood feud. If only I don't forget to say the right words before I fire, he thought. That's the main thing. If I don't forget to turn him the right way up and put his weapon by his head. That's the other main point. All the rest is easy, child's play.

However, the rules of the blood feud were only a small part of the Code, just a chapter. As weeks and months went by, Gjorg came to understand that the other part, which was concerned with everyday living and was not drenched with blood, was inextricably bound to the bloody part, so much so that no one could really tell where one part left off and the other began. The whole was so conceived that one begat the other, the stainless giving birth to the bloody, and the second to the first, and so on forever, from generation to generation.

In the distance, Gjorg saw a group of people on horseback. When they drew nearer, he made out a bride among them and he knew that the cavalcade consisted of the relatives of the bride who were taking her to her husband. Drenched by the rain, they seemed tired, and only the horses' bells lent a bit of gaiety to the little troop.

Gjorg stepped aside to let them pass. The horsemen, like himself, carried their weapons muzzle down to protect them from the rain. Looking at the parti-colored bundles which no doubt contained the bride's trousseau, he wondered in which corner, which box, which pocket, which embroidered waistcoat, the bride's parents had put the "trousseau bullet" with which, according to the Code, the bridegroom had the right to kill the bride if she should try to leave him. That thought mingled with the memory of his dead fiancée, whom he had not been able to marry because of her long illness. Whenever he saw a wedding party go by he could not help thinking about her, but on this day, oddly enough, his pain was lessened by a consoling thought: perhaps it was better for her that she had gone first to where he would soon overtake her, rather than to have before her a long life as a widow. And, as for that "trousseau bullet" that the parents were supposed to give the young husband so that he might kill his wife if she left him, he would certainly have tossed it into the ravine. Or perhaps he felt that way now that she was gone and the idea of killing someone who was no longer alive seemed to him as unreal as fighting with a ghost.

The relatives of the bride had disappeared from view before they faded from his mind. He thought of them, travelling along the road in accordance with all the rules, the chief of her kinsmen, the *Krushkapar,* at the end of the procession, the only difference being that now, under the veil, in the place of the bride, he imagined his betrothed. "A wedding day is never postponed," the Code said.

"Even if the bride is dying, the wedding party sets out, if necessary dragging her along to the bridegroom's house." Gjorg had often heard these words repeated during the sickness of his betrothed, when they talked at home of his approaching wedding day. "A wedding party sets out even if there is a death in the house. When the bride enters the house, the dead person leaves. Tears on one side, song on the other."

All these memories that he forced himself to entertain wearied him, and he tried not to think of anything. On either side of the road stretched long strips of fallows, and again nameless waste lands. Somewhere on the right he saw a watermill, then, farther off, a flock of sheep, and a church with its graveyard. He passed by them without turning his head, but that did not prevent him from remembering the portions of the Code that dealt with mills, flocks, churches and graves. "Priests have no part in the blood feud." "Among the graves of a family or a clan, no stranger's tomb may lie."

He was tempted to say, "That's enough," but could not find the strength to say it. He lowered his head and went on walking at the same pace. In the distance he could see the roof of an inn, further on a convent, then another flock of sheep, and beyond, smoke and perhaps a settlement; there were centuries-old laws for all these things. There was no escaping them. No one had ever succeeded in escaping them. And yet. . . . "Priests have no part in the blood feud," he repeated, citing one of the best known clauses of the Code. He was thinking of that as he was going along the stretch of road from which the convent was clearly visible, and the thought that only if he had been a priest would he have been spared by the *Kanun* got mixed up with thinking about nuns and the relations that people said they had with the young priests, and with the idea of possibly having an affair with a nun himself, but he suddenly remembered that nuns cropped their hair and he dismissed that fantasy. But I would have had to be a priest, he thought, so as not to be subject to the *Kanun*. But other sections of the Code were in fact applicable to priests, who were exempt only from the provisions that regulated the blood feud.

For a moment he felt as if he were trapped in bird-lime by the bloody part of the *Kanun*. Truly, that was the essential thing, and it was useless to console yourself that everyone was shackled by the same chains. Besides priests, there were numerous other people who escaped the rule of blood-law. He had already thought of that on another occasion. The world was divided into two parts: the one that fell under the blood-law, and the other that was outside that law.

Beyond the blood-law. He almost let out a sigh. What must life be like in such families? How did they get up in the mornings and how did they go to bed at night? It all seemed almost incredible, as remote perhaps as the life of the birds. And yet there were such houses. In fact, that had been the case of his own house seventy years ago, until that fateful autumn night when a man had knocked at their door.

Gjorg's father, who had it from his own father, had told him the story of their enmity with the Kryeqyqe family. It was a story marked by twenty-two graves on each side, forty-four in all, with the same set phrases to be spoken before the killings, but yet with more silence than speech, with sobs, with the death-rattle in the throat that chokes off a last wish, with three bardic songs, one of them forgotten, with the grave of a woman killed by accident whose death was indemnified according to the rules, with the men of both families immured in the tower of refuge*, with an attempt at reconciliation that failed at the last moment, with a killing that took place at a wedding with the granting of a short and a long truce, with a funeral dinner, with the cry, "So and so of the Berisha has fired at so and so of the Kryeqyqe," or the other way around, with torches, and comings and goings in the village and so on until that afternoon of March 17, when it had been Gjorg's turn to join the grisly dance.

And all this had begun seventy years ago, on a cold October night, when a man had knocked at their door, "Who was that man?" Gjorg had asked as a little boy, when for the first time he had heard the story of the knocking at the door. The question would be repeated many times in their house, at that time and later on, and no one would ever answer it. For no one had ever known who that man was. And even now, Gjorg could not believe that anyone had actually knocked at their door. It was easier for him to imagine that a ghost had knocked, or fate itself, rather than an unknown traveler.

The man, after knocking, had called from the gate and asked for shelter for the night. The head of the house, Gjorg's grandfather, had opened the door to him. They had welcomed him as was the custom, had brought him food and prepared him a bed, and early next morning, still according to custom, one of the family, his grandfather's younger brother, had escorted the unknown guest to the outer limits of the village. He had just left the man when he heard a shot. The stranger had fallen, dead, exactly at

---

* A tower without windows where a man who has killed may seek permanent refuge, and be maintained indefinitely with food and drink set just inside the door.

the border of the village lands. Now, according to the *Kanun*, when the guest whom you were accompanying is killed before your eyes, you are bound to avenge him. But if he had been struck down after you had turned your back, you were free of that obligation. The man who had been escorting his guest had in fact turned his back before the man had been hit; therefore it was not his responsibility to avenge him. But no one had seen it happen. It was very early in the morning and no one in the neighborhood could testify in the matter. Even so, his protector's word would have been believed, since the *Kanun* trusts a man's word, and it would have been regarded as established that the man who had accompanied his guest had taken leave of him and turned his back by the time the killing had occurred, if another obstacle had not arisen. That was the orientation of the victim's body. The committee that was formed at once to determine if the duty of avenging the unknown guest fell to the house of Berisha, considered everything minutely, and concluded at last that the Berisha were indeed the ones who must avenge him. The stranger had fallen face down with his head towards the village. For that reason, according to the Code, the Berisha who had given the stranger shelter and had fed him, had had the duty to protect him until he left the village lands, and must now avenge him.

The men of the Berisha family returned in silence from the wood where the commission had debated around the corpse for hours, and the women at the windows of the *kulla* had understood. Pale as wax, they had listened to the men's brief words, and had turned paler still. Yet no curse was murmured against the unknown guest who had brought death to their house, since a guest is sacred and, according to the custom, a mountaineer's house, before being his home and the home of his family, is the home of God and of guests.

On that same October day, it came out who it was that had shot the unknown traveller. It was a young man of the Kryeqyqe family, who had been on the watch for him a long time because the man had done him an injury in a cafe, in front of a woman, also unknown. And so, at the end of that October day, the Berisha found themselves in enmity with the Kryeqyqe. Gjorg's clan, which had hitherto lived in peace, was at last caught up by the great engine of the blood feud. Forty-four graves had been dug since then, and who knows how many are to come, and all because of the knocking at the gate on that autumn night.

Many times, when he was alone, when he let his mind stray, Gjorg had tried to imagine how the life of his clan would have run, had that late guest not knocked at the gate of their *kulla*, but at another gate. If, by magic, those knocks could be blanked out from reality, then, oh, then (and on this matter Gjorg thought the stuff of legend to be quite real), one would see the heavy stone slabs lifted from forty-four graves, and the forty-four dead men would rise, shake the earth from their faces, and return to the living; and with them would come the children who could not have been born, then the babies that those children could not bring into the world, and everything would be different, different. And all that would happen if, by enchantment, one could correct the course of things. Oh, if only he had stopped a little farther along. A little farther on. But he had stopped exactly where he had, and no one could change that anymore, no more than anyone could change the direction in which the victim had fallen, no more than anyone could ever change the rules of the ancient *Kanun*. . . . Without the knocking at the door, everything

33

would be so different that at times he was afraid to think of it, and he consoled himself with the notion that perhaps it had to happen this way, and that if life outside the whirlpool of blood might perhaps be more peaceful, by the same token it would be even more dull and meaningless. He tried to call to mind families that were not involved in the blood feud, and he found no special signs of happiness in them. It even seemed to him that, sheltered from that danger, they hardly knew the value of life, and were only the more unhappy for that. Whereas clans that were in the blood feud lived in a different order of days and seasons, accompanied as it were by an inner tremor; the people were more handsome, and the young men were in favor with the women. Even the two nuns whom he had first passed, when they had seen the black ribbon sewn to his sleeve that meant that he was searching for his death or that his death was searching for him, had looked at him strangely. But that was not the important thing; what was happening within him was the important thing. Something terrifying and majestic at the same time. He could not have explained it. He felt that his heart had leaped from his chest, and, opened up in that way, he was vulnerable, sensitive to everything, so that he might rejoice in anything, be cast down by anything, small or large, a butterfly, a leaf, boundless snow, or the depressing rain falling on that very day. But all that—and the sky itself might fall down upon him—his heart endured, and could endure even more.

He had been walking for hours, but except for a slight numbness in his knees, he was not at all tired. The rain was still falling, but the drops were sparse, as if someone had pruned away the clouds' roots. Gjorg was sure he had passed the boundaries of his own district and was journeying through another region. The country looked much the same; mountains raising their heads behind the shoulders of other mountains as if in frozen curiosity. He met a small party of mountaineers and asked them if he was on the right road for the Castle of Orosh, and how far off it might be. They told him he was going the right way, but that he would have to hurry if he wanted to arrive before nightfall. As they spoke, their eyes drifted towards the black ribbon on his sleeve and, perhaps because of the ribbon, they suggested again that he quicken his pace.

I'll hurry, I'll hurry, Gjorg said to himself, not without bitterness. Don't worry, I'll get there in time to pay the tax before nightfall. Without thinking, perhaps because of his sudden anger, or simply following automatically the advice of those strangers, he had indeed picked up his pace.

Now he was quite alone on the road, which crossed a narrow tableland furrowed by old watercourses. Around him the fields were desolate and untilled. He thought he heard the rumbling of distant thunder and looked up. A single airplane was flying slowly among the clouds. Wonderingly his eyes followed its flight for a while. He had heard that in the neighboring district a passenger plane flew by once a week, from Tirana to a far-off foreign country in Europe, but he had never seen it before.

When the airplane disappeared in the clouds, Gjorg felt a pain in his neck, and only then realized that he had stared at it for a long time. The plane left a great emptiness behind it, and Gjorg sighed unawares. Suddenly he felt hungry. He looked around for a fallen tree trunk or stone to sit upon and eat the bread and goat cheese he had brought along, but on either side of the road there was only the naked earth, dried watercourses, and nothing more. I'll go on a little further, he said to himself.

And after another half-hour of walking, he made out the roof of an inn in the distance. He traversed almost at a run the stretch of road leading to it, stopped for a moment before the door, then went into the building. It was an ordinary inn, like all the others in the mountain districts, with no signboard, the roof steep-pitched, smelling of straw, and with a large common room. On either side of a long oaken table with many scorch marks, some customers were sitting on chairs of the same wood. Two of them were bending down to bowls of beans, eating greedily. Another stared vacantly at the planks of the table, his head supported by his hands.

As he sat down on one of the chairs, Gjorg felt the muzzle of his rifle touch the floor. He slipped the weapon from his shoulder, set it down across his thighs, and, with a shake of his head, threw back the soaked hood of his cloak. He felt the presence of other people behind him, and only then noticed that on either side of the stairway that led to the upper storey, other mountaineers were sitting on black sheepskins and woolen packs. Some of them, leaning against the wall, were eating corn bread that they dipped in whey. Gjorg thought that he would get up from the table, and like them, take out his bread and his cheese from his bag, but at that moment the smell of beans reached his nostrils and at once he wanted terribly a plate of hot beans. His father had given him a coin, but it was not clear to Gjorg whether he could really spend it or if he was supposed to bring it back unspent. Meanwhile, the innkeeper, whom Gjorg had not been aware of until then, appeared before him.

"Going to the *Kulla* of Orosh?" he asked. "Where are you from?"

"From Brezftoht."

36

"Then you must be hungry. Would you like to have something?"

The innkeeper was skinny and deformed. Gjorg thought the man must be a sharper, because while saying, "Would you like to have something?" instead of looking him in the eye, he stared at the black band on Gjorg's sleeve, as if to say, "If you're about to pay five hundred *groschen* for the murder you did, the world won't come to an end if you spend a couple of them in my inn."

"Would you like to have something?" the innkeeper asked again, turning his eyes from Gjorg's sleeve at last but still not looking at his face but at some place off to the side.

"A plate of beans," said Gjorg. "How much will it be? I've got my own bread."

He blushed, but he had to ask the question. Not for anything would he spend any part of the money set aside for the blood tax.

"A quarter *groschen*," said the innkeeper.

Gjorg breathed a sigh of relief. The innkeeper turned away, and when he came back a moment later with a wooden bowl full of beans in his hand, Gjorg saw that he had a squint. As if to forget, he bent his head over the bowl of beans and began to eat quickly.

"Would you like coffee?" the innkeeper asked, when he came to take away the empty bowl.

Gjorg looked at him bewildered. His eyes seemed to say, don't tempt me. I may have five hundred *groschen* in my purse but I'd rather give you my head (Lord, he thought, that's just what it will cost me, my head thirty days from now, and even before thirty days, twenty-eight days), before time, than one *groschen* from the purse that's

37

owing to the *Kulla* of Orosh. But the innkeeper, as if he guessed what was in Gjorg's mind, added:

"It's very cheap. Ten cents."

Gjorg nodded impatiently. The innkeeper, moving awkwardly between the chairs and the table, cleared away dishes, brought fresh ones, and then disappeared again, finally coming back with a cup of coffee in his hand.

Gjorg was still sipping his coffee when a small group entered the inn. From the stir their arrival caused, from the turning of heads and by the way the lame innkeeper behaved in their presence, he understood that the newcomers must be well-known in the district. One of them, the man who came at once into the center of the room, was very short, with a cold, pallid face. After him came a man dressed like a townsman, but very oddly, with a checked jacket, and his breeches stuffed into his boots. The third man had a face whose features seemed somehow blunted and whose eyes rained scorn. But it was clear at once that everybody's attention was centered upon the short man.

"Ali Binak, Ali Binak," people began to whisper around Gjorg. His eyes widened, as if he could scarcely believe that there, in the same inn as himself, was the famous interpreter of the *Kanun*, of whom he had heard since he was a child.

The innkeeper, with his odd sidling walk, invited the small party into an adjacent room, evidently reserved for distinguished guests.

The short man mumbled a brief greeting to no one in particular, and without turning his head either to the right or to the left, he followed the innkeeper. While appearing to be aware of his fame, he was, surprisingly, quite without the haughty bearing common among men of small stature who have a sense of their own importance; on the

38

contrary, his movements, his face, and especially his eyes, suggested the calm of a man without illusions.

The newcomers had disappeared into the other room, but the whispering on their account had not stopped. Gjorg had finished his coffee, but while he knew that time was important now, he was pleased to be sitting there, listening to the lively comments on every hand. Why had Ali Binak come? he wondered. No doubt to settle some complex case. Besides, he had been dealing with such things all his life. They called him from Province to Province and from Banner to Banner to ask his opinion in difficult cases, when the elders were divided among themselves over the interpretation of the Code. Of the hundreds of interpreters in the limitless space of the north country *rrafsh**, there were no more than ten as famous as Ali Binak. So that it was not for nothing that he went to one place or another. This time, too, someone said, he had come about a complicated boundary question that had to be settled promptly, tomorrow, in the neighboring Banner. But who was the other, the man with the light-colored eyes? That's right, who was he? They said he was a doctor whom Ali Binak often brought with him in thorny affairs, especially when it was a matter of reckoning up wounds to be paid for with fines. Well, if that was the case, Ali Binak hadn't come about a boundary dispute but for some other reason, since of course a doctor had no business with boundaries. Perhaps they had misunderstood all along. Some said that he was in fact here about another matter, very complicated, that had come up a few days ago in the village beyond the plateau. In an exchange of shots because of a quarrel, a woman who happened to be there, between the rivals, had been killed in the cross-

---
* Plateau, in Albanian.

fire. She was pregnant, and with a man-child, as was proved after the baby had been extracted. The village elders, it appeared, were very perplexed in deciding who had the duty of taking revenge for the infant. Could it be that Ali Binak had come to clear up this very case?

But the other one in his odd get-up, who was he? Just as with all the other questions, there was an answer to this one. He was a sort of public servant whose business was measuring land, but he had the Devil knows what kind of name to him that ended in "meter," the kind of word you can't pronounce without twisting your tongue, geo, geo. . . . that's it, *geometer*.

Oh, then it must be about the boundary business, if this geometer, or whatever you call him, is here.

Gjorg wanted to stay and listen a while longer, the more so because there was every reason to think that people would be telling other kinds of stories at the inn, but if he lingered, he risked not getting to the castle in time. He stood up suddenly, so as not to be tempted again, paid for the beans and the coffee, and was about to leave; at the last moment he remembered to ask for directions once more.

"You take the highroad," the innkeeper said, "then, when you come to the Graves of the Wedding Guests, at the place where the road forks, make sure you go right, not left. You hear, the right fork."

When Gjorg went outside, the rain had fallen off still more, but the air was very damp. The day was as cloudy as the morning had been, and just as there are certain women whose age you cannot guess, there was no way to tell what time it was.

Gjorg went on, trying to think of nothing at all. The road stretched endlessly with grey wasteland on either hand. Once his eye fell on some half-sunken graves scattered along the roadside. He thought that these must be the Graves of the Wedding Guests. Then, since the road did not fork there, he decided that those graves must be further on. And so it turned out. They appeared a quarter of an hour later, and they were sunken like the others, but even more dismal, and covered with moss. As he passed them he imagined that the party of wedding guests he had met with that morning had simply turned round and come back to bury themselves in this cemetery and take up their abode here forever.

He took the right fork of the road, as the innkeeper had advised, and, moving on, he had to force himself not to turn his head and look at the old graves again. For a time, he managed to walk without a thought in his head, yet with a curious sense of being at one with the humped shapes of the mountains and the clouds about him. He was not aware how long he had been going on in that indolent way. He would have liked to go on in that way forever, but suddenly there rose up before him something that took his mind off the rocks and mists at once. It was the ruins of a house.

As he went by it, he looked out of the corner of his eye at the great heap of stones; rain and wind had long ago effaced the marks of the fire, replacing them with a sickly grey tint the sight of which seemed to help you get rid of a sob long imprisoned in your throat.

Gjorg walked on, looking sidelong at the ruins. With a sudden jump he vaulted the shallow roadside ditch and in two or three strides reached the pile of burned stone. For an instant he was still, and then, like someone who, confronted by the body of a dying man, tries to find the wound and guess what weapon has brought death near, he went to one of the corners of the house, bent down,

41

moved a few stones, did the same thing with the other three corners, and having seen that the cornerstones had been pulled out of their beds, he knew that this was a house that had broken the laws of hospitality. Besides burning them down, there was this further treatment reserved for those houses in which the most serious crime had been committed, according to the *Kanun*: the betrayal of the guest who was under the protection of the *bessa*.

Gjorg remembered the punishment meted out some years ago in his village when the *bessa* had been violated. The murderer had been shot by the assembled men of the village, and he had been declared unworthy of being avenged. Then, without taking into account that the people who lived in the house were not guilty of the murder, that house, in which a guest had been killed in violation of the *bessa*, was burned. The head of the household himself was the first to scatter the firebrands and take the axe to the building, shouting, "May I wash clean my sins against the village and the Banner." At his back, with torch and axe, came all the men of the village. After that, for years, nothing could be handed to the head of the house except with the left hand passed under one's thigh, to remind him that he should have avenged the blood of his guest. For it was a settled thing that one could atone for the blood of a father, of a brother—even one's child—but never for the blood of a guest.

Who knows what treacherous act was committed in this house, he said to himself, dislodging a couple of stones with his foot. They rolled away with a dull sound. He looked around him to see if there were other houses there, but saw nothing but another ruin twenty paces away. What can that mean, he wondered. Mechanically, he

42

rushed to that other ruin, went around it, and saw the same thing at the four corners. All the cornerstones had been torn away. Could it be that the whole village had been punished? But when he came upon still another ruin further on, he was convinced that that must be so. He had heard a few years ago of a village far away that had violated the *bessa*, and had been punished for it by the Banner. A go-between had been killed during a dispute about the boundaries between two villages. The Banner ruled that the village in which he had been killed had the duty to avenge him. And the village having been so thoughtless as not to avenge him, it had been decided that the village must be destroyed.

Gjorg walked softly, like a shadow, from one ruin to the next. Who had that man been who had involved a whole village in his death? Those deaf ruins were dreadful. A bird whose sound, Gjorg knew, was only heard at night, said, "Or, or," and remembering that he had little time in which to reach the *Kulla*, he looked for the highway again. The bird's cry rent the silence again, far away now, and Gjorg asked again who might that man be who had been betrayed in this ill-fated village. "Or-or!" came the answer, which to his ear seemed somewhat like his name, "Gjorg-Gjorg." He smiled, telling himself, "Now you're hearing voices," and he turned towards the road.

A little later on, having resumed his journey, as if to jettison the feeling of oppression that the ruined village had left with him, he made an effort to call to mind the mildest penalties prescribed by the Code. Betraying one's guest was most unusual, and therefore the burning of houses, and still more the razing of whole villages, was rarer still. He remembered that less serious offenses meant the banishment of the guilty party and all his kin from the Banner.

Gjorg noticed that as the penalties came thronging to his imagination, he walked faster, as if he wanted to escape them. The punishments were many: ostracism—the guilty man was segregated forever (debarred from funerals, weddings, and the right to borrow flour); withdrawal of the right to cultivate his land, accompanied by the destruction of his fruit trees; enforced fasting within the family; the ban on bearing arms whether on his shoulder or at his belt for one or two weeks; being chained or under house arrest; taking away from the master or mistress of the house his or her authority in the family.

The possibility of the punishment that he might incur within his own family had tormented him for a long time. And that suffering had begun the moment when his turn came to avenge his brother's death.

He could not put out of mind that icy morning in January when his father had called him to the great room on the upper storey of the house so that they could talk privately. The day was particularly bright, the sky and the new-fallen snow were dazzling, the world shone like glass, and with a kind of crystal madness it seemed that it might begin to slip at any moment and shatter into thousands of fragments. It was that sort of morning when his father reminded him of his duty. Gjorg was sitting by the window, listening to his father who spoke to him of blood. The whole world was stained with it. It shone red upon the snow, pools of it spread and stiffened everywhere. Then Gjorg understood that all that red was in his own eyes. He listened to his father, his head down. And in the days that followed, for the first time, without knowing why, he began to tell over in his head all the punishments that a disobedient member of the family might incur. He

44

did not want to admit to himself that he hated to kill a man. The hatred for the Kryeqyqe family that his father was trying to kindle in his heart on that January morning could not prevail over that brilliant light. Gjorg did not understand then that if the fire of hatred could not strike fire in him, one reason was that the man who tried to kindle it, his father, was himself ice-cold. It would seem that long ago, during that endless feud, all hatred had slowly cooled, or perhaps had never existed. His father talked on in vain. . . . Gjorg fearfully, almost in terror, understood that he could not hate the man he was supposed to kill. And when, in the days that followed, his mind would wander only to come back to the list of punishments in store for a disobedient member of the household, he began to understand that he was mentally preparing himself not to shed blood. But at the same time, he knew that it was useless to let his thoughts run on the punishments that his family might impose. Like everyone else he knew that for any breach of the rules of the blood feud there were other penalties, much more grim.

The second time they spoke about avenging the dead, his father's tone was harsher. The day was quite different, too. It was wan, miserable, without rain or even fog, not to speak of lightning, which would have been too much luxury for that washed-out sky. Gjorg tried to avoid his father's eyes, but at last his own were caught in that stare as in a trap.

"Look," his father said, nodding at the shirt hanging on the wall in front of them.

Gjorg turned his head in that direction. He felt that the veins in his neck grated as if they were rusty.

"The blood is turning yellow," his father said. "The dead man cries out for vengeance."

The blood had in fact yellowed on the cloth. Or rather it

45

had turned a rusty color like that of the first water flowing from a faucet that has not been used for a long time.

"Gjorg, you're putting it off," his father went on. "Our honor, but yours especially. . . ."

"Two fingers-breadth of honor have been stamped on our forehead by almighty God." In the weeks that followed, Gjorg repeated to himself hundreds of times the words of the Code that his father had recited to him that day. "Whiten or further besmirch your dirty face, as you please. It is up to you to be a man or not."

Am I free? he asked himself as he went upstairs to think about it alone on the *kulla*'s second storey. The punishments his father could subject him to for this or that infraction were nothing compared to the risk of losing his honor. Two fingers-breadth of honor on our forehead. He touched his forehead with his hand, as if to find the exact place where his honor might be. And why should it be just there? he wondered. It was only a phrase that went from mouth to mouth and was never quite swallowed. Now at last he had fathomed its meaning. Honor had its seat in the middle of your forehead because that was the place where the bullet must strike your man. "Good shot," the old men said when someone faced his man squarely and hit him right in the forehead. Or "Bad shot" when the bullet pierced the stomach or struck a limb, not to mention the back.

Whenever Gjorg climbed to the upper storey to look at Mehill's shirt, he felt his forehead burning. The blood-stains on the cloth faded more and more. If warm weather came, they would turn yellow. Then people would begin to hand his coffee cup to him and to his kin under the leg. In the eyes of the *Kanun*, he would be a dead man.

There was no way out. Bearing the punishments, or any

46

other sacrifice, would not save him. Coffee below the knee—that frightened him more than anything else—was waiting for him somewhere along the way. Every door was closed to him, except one. "The offense can be atoned for only through the Code," the Code itself said. Only the murder of a member of the Kryeqyqe clan could open a door to him. And so, one day last spring, he decided to lie in ambush for his man.

From that moment the whole house sprang to life. The silence that had stifled it was suddenly filled with music. And its grim walls seemed to soften.

He would already have done his duty, and he would be at peace, now, shut up in the tower of refuge, or still more at peace under the earth, had not something happened. From a far-off Banner, an aunt of theirs who had married there came unexpectedly. Anxious, distraught, she had crossed seven or eight mountain ranges and as many valleys to stop the bloodshed. Gjorg was the last man in the family after his father, she said. "Look, they'll kill Gjorg, and then they'll kill one of the Kryeqyqe, then it will be the turn of Gjorg's father, and the Berisha family will be extinct. Don't do it. Don't let the oak tree wither. Ask for the right to pay the blood-money instead."

At first nobody would even listen, then they fell silent, they let her speak, and at last there was a lull in which they neither agreed nor disagreed with what she proposed. They were tired, but Gjorg's aunt gave no sign of tiring. Keeping up the struggle day and night, sleeping now in this house and now in that, sometimes with her cousins and sometimes with her immediate family, she finally gained her point: after seventy years of death and mourning, the Berishas decided to seek blood settlement with the Kryeqyqes.

47

The request for blood settlement—so rare in the mountains—caused a sensation in the village and throughout the Banner. Everything was done to ensure that the prescriptions of the Code were scrupulously observed. The arbiters, together with friends and kinsmen of the Berisha, who were called the "masters of the blood," went to the home of the murderer, that is, to the Kryeqyqe, to eat the blood-compensation meal. So they ate the noon meal with the murderer in keeping with the custom, and settled the blood price that the Kryeqyqes would have to pay. After this it only remained for Gjorg's father, the master of the blood, to carve a cross with hammer and chisel on the murderer's door and for them to exchange a drop of blood with each other, at which point the reconciliation would be regarded as having been established forever. But that money never came, for an aged uncle kept the business from being settled in that way. After the meal, while the men, according to custom, were going through every room in the house, stamping their feet, a rite signifying that the last shadow of the feud must be driven out of every corner of the house, suddenly Gjorg's old uncle shouted, "No!" He was a quiet old man who had never called attention to himself in the clan, and certainly the last person among those present of whom one might expect such a thing. Everyone was dumbfounded, and every eye, every neck that had been raised at the same time that their feet had risen to stamp again on the floor, all fell softly, as if on cotton batting. "No," the old uncle said again. Then the priest who was there as the chief mediator waved his hand. He said, "More blood must flow."

Gjorg, who for a time had been almost ignored, now found himself once more with all eyes upon him. Yet with the return of his old trouble, from which he had escaped

48

momentarily, he felt a certain satisfaction. It seemed that this satisfaction came from the sense that everyone was interested in him. Now he felt that he could not say which life was better, a quiet life dusted over with forgetfulness and excluded from the machinery of the blood feud, or that other life, the life of danger, but with a lightning bolt of grief that ran through it like a quivering seam. He had tasted both, and if someone had said to him now, "Choose one or the other," Gjorg would certainly have hesitated. Perhaps it took years to get used to peace, just as it had taken so many years to get used to its absence. The mechanism of the blood feud was such that even as it freed you, it kept you bound to it in spirit for a long time.

In the days that followed the failure of the attempted settlement, when in the sky that had been empty for a little while the clouds of danger massed again, Gjorg asked himself often whether that attempt at reconciliation had been for the best or not, and he had no answer. The advantage had been that it had given him another year of free life, but in other respects it had been disastrous in that now he had to reaccustom himself to the life from which he had broken away, to the idea of killing someone. Soon he would have to become a justicer, as the Code called those who killed to avenge the dead. The justicers were a kind of vanguard of the clan, the ones who carried out the killings, but also the first to be killed in the blood feud. When it was the turn of the opposing clan to wreak vengeance, they tried to do so by killing the other clan's justicer. Only if that were not possible would they mark down another man in place of him. During seventy years of enmity for the Kryeqyqe family, the Berishas had produced twenty-two justicers, most of whom had been killed by a bullet later. The justicers were the flower of a

49

clan, its marrow, and its chief memorial. Many things were forgotten in the life of the clan, men and events alike covered with dust; only the justicers, tiny, inextinguishable flames on the graves of the clan, were never effaced from its memory.

Summer came and went, more swiftly than in any other year. The Berishas hurried to finish the work in the fields, so that after the killing they could shut themselves up in their *kulla*. Gjorg experienced a kind of quiet bitterness, something like what a young man might feel on the eve of his wedding day.

At last, at the end of October, he fired at Zef Kryeqyqe, without managing to kill him. He only wounded him in the jawbone. Then came the doctors of the Code, whose business it was to assess the fine to be paid by the man who inflicted a wound, and since this was a head wound, they valued it at three purses of *groschen*, which amounted to half the price of a killing. This meant that the Berishas could choose either to pay the fine or to regard the wound as representing one-half of their vengeance. In the latter case, if they did not pay the fine but treated the wound as a part settlement of the blood that was owed, then they had no right to kill a Kryeqyqe, because half the blood had already been taken. They had the right to inflict a wound only.

Naturally, the Berishas did not agree to reckon the wound as a part payment. Though the fine was heavy, they dug down into their savings and paid it so that the blood account remained intact.

As long as the matter of the fine to be paid for the wound was still going on, Gjorg saw that his father's eyes were darkened by a veil of scorn and bitterness. They seemed to say, not only did you draw out the business of taking revenge for so long, but now you're driving us to rack and ruin.

Gjorg himself felt that all this had been brought about by his hesitation, which had made his hand tremble at the last moment. To tell the truth, he could not tell if his hand had really trembled when he took aim, or if he had purposely dropped the front sight of his weapon from the man's forehead to the lower portion of his face.

All this was followed by apathy. Life seemed to mark time. The wounded man suffered at home for a long while. The bullet had broken his jawbone, they said, and infection had set in. The winter was long and more dismal than ever before. Over the placid snow (the old men said that no one could remember the snow being so quiet—not one avalanche), the wind made a slight whistling sound as unchanging as the snow. Zef of the Kryeqyqe, the sole object of Gjorg's life, went on languishing in bed, and Gjorg felt like a man out of work, wandering about uselessly.

It really felt as if that winter would never end. And the very moment when they learned that the wounded man was getting better, Gjorg fell ill. Sick at heart, he would have borne martyrdom so as not to have to take to his bed before he had carried out his mission, but it was quite impossible. He turned pale as wax, kept on his feet as long as he could, then collapsed. He was bedridden for two months while Zef Kryeqyqe, taking advantage of Gjorg's illness, began to walk about the village free as air. From the corner of the second storey of the *kulla* where he lay, Gjorg looked out, scarcely thinking at all, at the patch of landscape framed by the window. Beyond that stretched the world whitened by the snow, a world to which nothing bound him anymore. For a long time he had felt

51

himself a stranger in that world, absolutely superfluous, and if outside his window people sill expected anything of him, it was only in terms of the murder he was to do.

For hours on end he looked scornfully at the snow-covered ground, as if to say, yes, I'll go out there, I'll go out quickly to spill that bit of blood. The thought haunted him so much that sometimes he thought he really saw a small red stain take shape in the heart of that endless white.

In the first days of March he felt a little better, and in the second week of the month he left his bed. When he stepped outside his legs were shaky. Nobody imagined that in his condition, still dizzy from his illness, his face white as a sheet, he would go out to lie in ambush for his man. Perhaps that was why Zef of the Kryeqyqe, knowing that his enemy was still ill, had been taken unawares.

At moments the rain fell so sparsely that one would imagine it must stop, but suddenly it started up again better than ever. By that time it was afternoon and Gjorg felt his legs getting numb. The gray day was the same; only the district was different. Gjorg could tell because the mountaineers he met wore different clothing. The small villages were farther and farther from the highroad. In places the bronze of a church bell glinted weakly in the distance. Then for miles the landscape was empty.

He met fewer and fewer travelers. Gjorg asked again about the *Kulla* of Orosh. First, people told him it was quite close by, then, further on, when he thought he must really be drawing near, they told him it was still a long way. And each time the passers-by pointed in the same direction, in the distance where sight was lost in the mist.

Two or three times Gjorg imagined that night was falling, but it turned out that he was mistaken. It was still that endless afternoon in which the villages drew further away from the highway as if they meant to hide from the road and from the world. Once more he asked if the castle was still far off, and he was told that it was very near now. The last traveler even stretched his hand in the direction where it was supposed to be.

"Will I get there before nightfall?" Gjorg asked him.

"I think so," he said. "Just around nightfall."

Gjorg set off again. He was sinking with fatigue. Sometimes he was ready to believe that the evening, in delaying, was keeping the *Kulla* far off, and sometimes on the contrary, it was the remoteness of the *Kulla* that kept the evening suspended, without letting it settle on the earth.

Once he thought he could make out the silhouette of the *Kulla* through the fog, but the dark mass proved to be a convent, like the one he had seen in the morning of that long day. Farther along, he felt once again that he was close to the *Kulla*, and even thought that at last he could see it clearly on the top of a steep hill, but going on he saw that it was not the *Kulla* of Orosh, it was not a building at all, but a mere rag of fog darker than the others.

When he found himself alone again on the highroad, he felt all hope of ever reaching the castle fail within him. The emptiness of the road on either side seemed emptier still because of the shrubby growth that had sprung up there as if with an evil intention. What is the matter, Gjorg thought. Now, he could see no villages at all, no matter how far back from the road, and the worst of it was his conviction that they would never appear again.

Walking along, he raised his head from time to time, looking for the *Kulla* on the horizon, and again he thought he saw it, but scarcely believing that he did. From the time of his childhood, he had heard about the princely castle that had guarded for centuries men's adherence to the Code, but for all that he did not know what it looked like, nor anything more about it. The people of the Plateau simply called it Orok, and it was impossible to imagine the appearance of the place from their stories. And now that Gjorg caught sight of it in the distance, not believing that it was really the castle, he could not make out its shape. In the fog its silhouette seemed neither high nor low, and sometimes he thought it must be quite spread out and sometimes he thought it a compact mass. Gjorg found that it gave the impression that the road climbed up in switch-backs, and that his changing point of view made the building change continually. But even when he was quite close, he could make out nothing distinctly. He was sure that it must be the castle and he was certain that it was not. At one moment he thought he saw a single roof covering various buildings, and at another, several roofs covering a single building. Its appearance changed as he approached. Now he thought he saw a castle-keep rising amidst a number of structures that seemed to be outbuildings. But when he had walked on a bit farther, the main tower disappeared and he saw only those outbuildings. Then these too began in turn to break up, and when he came closer still, he saw that they were not fortified towers, but dwellings of some kind, and in part not even that but perhaps galleries, more or less abandoned. There was no one about. Did I take the wrong road, he wondered. But just then a man appeared before him.

"The death tax?" the man asked, glancing surreptitiously at Gjorg's right sleeve, and without waiting for an answer, he extended his arm towards one of the galleries.

Gjorg turned in that direction. He felt that his legs would not hold him up. Before him was a wooden door, a very old one. He turned round, as if to ask the man who had spoken to him if he should go in there, but the man was gone. He looked at the door for a moment before making up his mind to knock. The wood was all rotten, bristling with all sorts of nail-heads and bits of iron carelessly hammered in, mostly askew and serving no purpose. All that metal had become one with the ancient wood, like the fingernails of an old man's hand.

He started to knock, but he noticed that the door, though punched and stuck with so many pieces of iron, had no knocker, nor even any trace of a lock. Only then did he see that the door was ajar, and he did something he had never done in his life before: he pushed open a door, without first calling out: "Oh, master of the house!"

The long room was in semi-darkness. At first he thought it was empty. Then he made out a fire in one corner. Not much of a fire, and fed with damp wood that gave out more smoke than flame. Some men were waiting in that room. He smelled the odor of the heavy woolen cloth of their cloaks before he could see their forms, sitting on wooden stools or squatting in the corners.

Gjorg too huddled in a corner, putting his rifle between his knees. Little by little his eyes grew accustomed to the dim light. The acrid smoke gave him a bitter taste in his throat. He began to see black ribbons on their sleeves and he understood that, like him, they had come there to pay the death tax. There were four. A little later he thought he saw five. But less than a quarter of an hour later he thought there were four again. What he had taken for the fifth man was only a log stood on end, who could tell why, in the darkest corner.

"Where are you from?" asked the man nearest him.

Gjorg told him the name of his village.

Outside, night had fallen. To Gjorg it seemed to have come down all at once, as soon as he had crossed the threshold of the long room, like the wall of a ruin that collapses as soon as you have left its shadow.

"Not all that far, then," the man said. "I've had to travel two days and a half without stopping."

Gjorg did not know what to say.

Someone came in having pushed open the door, which creaked. He carried an armload of wood that he threw on the fire. The wood was wet and the flickering light went out. But a moment later, the man, who seemed to be crippled, lit an oil lamp and hung it on one of the many nails hammered into the wall. The yellow light, enfeebled by the soot on the lamp-chimney, tried in vain to reach the far corners of the room.

No one spoke. The man left the room, and a moment later another man came in. He resembled the first one, but he carried nothing in his hands. He looked at them all as if he was counting them (two or three times he looked at the log, as if to make sure that it was not a man) and he went out. A little later he came back with an earthen pot. After him came another man carrying bowls and two loaves of cornbread. He set down before each man a bowl and some bread, and the other poured bean soup from the pot.

"You're lucky," Gjorg's neighbor said. "You came just at the time when they're serving a meal. Otherwise you'd have to tighten your belt until dinnertime tomorrow."

"I brought along a little bread and cheese with me," said Gjorg.

"Why? At the castle they serve meals twice a day to those who come to pay the blood tax."

"I didn't know," said Gjorg, swallowing a great mouthful of bread. The cornbread was hard, but he was very hungry.

Gjorg felt some metal thing fall across his knees. It was his neighbor's tobacco tin.

"Have a smoke," he said.

"How long have you been here?"

"Since noon."

Although Gjorg said nothing, the other man seemed to have guessed that he was surprised.

"Why are you surprised? There are people who have been waiting since yesterday."

"Really?" Gjorg exclaimed. "I thought I could pay the money tonight and set out for my village tomorrow."

"No. If you get to pay before tomorrow evening, you'll be lucky. You might have to wait two days, if not three."

"Three days? How can that be?"

"The *Kulla* is in no hurry to collect the blood tax."

The door creaked and the man who had brought the pot of bean soup came in again. He picked up the empty bowls, stirred up the fire as he went by it, and went out again. Gjorg's eyes followed him.

"Are these people the prince's servants?" he asked his neighbor in a low voice.

The other man shrugged his shoulders.

"I can't rightly say. It seems that they are distant cousins of the family who also work as servants."

"Really?"

"Did you see those buildings round about? A lot of families live in them who have blood ties with the captain. Those people are both guards and officials. Did you see how they dress? Neither like mountain people nor townsfolk."

"Yes, that's true," Gjorg said.

"Roll yourself another smoke," said the other man, reaching him the tobacco tin.

"No, thank you," said Gjorg. "I don't smoke much."

57

"When did you kill your man?"

"The day before yesterday."

You could hear the sound of falling rain outside.

"This winter's dragging on."

"Yes, that's true. It's been a long one."

Far off, from deep within the group of buildings, perhaps from the main tower itself, there came the sharp grating of a gate. It was one side of a pair of heavy gates opening, or closing, and the grating noise went on for a time. It was followed at once by a cry that was like the cry of a night bird, and that might just as well have been a sentinel's cry, or a shout of farewell to a friend. Gjorg huddled deeper into his corner. He could not convince himself that he was at Orosh.

The creaking of the door cut through his drowsiness. For the third time Gjorg opened his eyes and saw the crippled man enter with an armload of wood in his arms. After throwing the wood on the fire, he turned up the wick of the oil lamp. The logs dripped water, and Gjorg thought that it must still be raining.

In the lamplight, Gjorg could see that nobody in the room was sleeping. His back was cold, but something kept him from moving nearer the fire. Besides, he had the feeling that it gave no warmth. The wavering light, splashed here and there with black stains, deepened the silence that hung over the waiting men.

Two or three times it occurred to Gjorg that all these men had killed, and that each had his story. But those stories were locked deep within them. It was not just chance that in the glow of the fire their mouths, and even more their jaws, looked as if they had the shape of certain antique locks. All during his journey to the *Kulla*, Gjorg had been terrified by the thought that somebody might ask him about his own story. And his fear was at its worst when he had entered this long room, though once he was inside something had persuaded him that he was out of danger. Perhaps he found reassurance in the stiff manner of those who were already there, or even from the log, that the newcomer mistook for a man before realizing his mistake, or on the contrary, took it for a log and then, smiling at what he supposed to be an error, greeted it as a man—only to find out the truth later. And at this point, Gjorg was inclined to think that the log had been put there for just that purpose.

As soon as the wet logs had been thrown upon the fire by the crippled man, they began to crackle. Gjorg took a deep breath. Outside, the night had certainly grown darker. In the distance, the north wind whistled low as it skimmed over the earth. He was surprised to find that he felt the need to say something. But besides that he was surprised by a very strange feeling indeed. It seemed to him that the jaws of the men around him were slowly changing their shape. Their stories were rising in their throats, and they began to chew them the way cattle chew their cud during the cold winter nights. Now their stories began to drip from their mouths. How many days now since the killing? Four. And you?

Little by little the stories came out from under the coarse cloth of their cloaks, like blackbeetles, wandered out quietly, passed one another. What will you do with your thirty-day truce?

What will I do? Gjorg wondered. Nothing.

Sometimes he thought he would be stuck forever in that damp room, by that fire that never really burst into flame, that made you shiver rather than warmed you, and with those black bugs shining on the floor.

When would they call him to pay his tax? Since the time he had come there, only one man had been called out. Would he have to wait for days and days? And what if a week passed and nobody called him out? What if they did not take him in at all?

The door opened and a stranger came in. One could see that he had come from far away. The fire gave a couple of contemptuous flickers, just enough light to show that he was all muddy and drenched to the skin, and left him in the semi-darkness, like all the others.

The man, looking confused and bewildered, found a seat right by the log of wood. Gjorg watched him out of the corner of his eye, to see how he himself had looked when he had come in a few hours ago. The man threw back his hood and let his chin sink to his raised knees. His story, obviously, buried deep inside him, was still far from his throat. Or perhaps it had not entered his body but was still outside, on his icy hands with which he had done murder, and that now stirred nervously about his knees.

CHAPTER III

The carriage went on climbing the mountain road at a lively pace. It was a rubber-tired vehicle of the kind used in the capital for excursions, or as a hackney coach. Its seats were upholstered in black velvet, but there was also something velvety about its very aspect. Perhaps that was why it rolled along on that rather poor mountain road much more easily than one would have expected, and perhaps it would have done so more quietly still but for the panting of the horses and the clopping of their hooves, which the upholstery could do nothing to muffle.

Holding his wife's hand, Bessian Vorpsi moved his head close to the window to make sure that the small town they had left half an hour before, the last one at the foot of the *Rrafsh*, the high plateau of the north, had disappeared from view. Now, before them and on either side there stretched away heathland on a slight slope, a rather strange piece of country, neither plain, nor mountain nor plateau. The mountains, properly speaking, had not yet begun, but one felt their looming shadow, and it seemed that it was that very shadow which while rejecting any connection between the plateau and the mountain world, kept it from being classed as a plain. So it was a border region, barren and almost uninhabited.

Now and then droplets of rain pearled the glass of the carriage window.

"The Accursed Mountains," he said softly, with a slight tremor in his voice, as if he were greeting a vision that he had been expecting for a very long time. He felt that the name, with its solemnity, had made an impression on his wife, and he took a certain satisfaction in it.

Her face came closer, and he breathed in the perfume of her neck.

"Where are they?"

He nodded ahead, and then he pointed, but in that direction she saw nothing but a heavy layer of mist.

"You can't see anything yet," he explained. "We're far away from them."

She left her hand in her husband's and leaned back into the velvet cloth of her seat. The jostling of the carriage sent the newspaper in which they were mentioned, and which they had bought in the small town a little before their departure, sliding to the floor, but neither of them moved to pick it up. She smiled vaguely, recalling the title of the short piece announcing their trip: "Sensation: The writer, Bessian Vorpsi, and his young bride are spending their honeymoon on the Northern Plateau!"

The article was rather vague. You could not tell whether the author, a certain A.G. (could that be their acquaintance, Adrian Guma?) was in favor of the trip or was being slightly ironic about it.

She herself, when her fiancé had announced it to her two weeks before the wedding, had thought the idea pretty bizarre. Don't be surprised at anything, her friends had told her. If you marry a man who's a bit odd, you have to expect surprises. But at bottom we have to say you're very lucky.

And in fact she was happy. During the last days before the wedding, in the half-fashionable, half-artistic circles of Tirana, people talked about nothing but their honeymoon trip. Her friends envied her and told her: You'll be escaping the world of reality for the world of legend, literally the world of epic that scarcely exists anymore. And they would go on talking about fairies, mountain nymphs, bards, the last Homeric hymns in the world, and the *Kanun*, terrifying but so majestic. Others shrugged their shoulders at all this enthusiasm, hinting discreetly at their astonishment, which was aroused particularly by the question of comfort, the more so since this was a honeymoon trip, something that called for certain conveniences, whereas, in the mountains the weather was still quite cold, and those epic *kullas* were of stone. On the other hand, there were others—few in number—who listened to all those opinions with a rather amused air, as if to say, "Right, go on up north among the mountain nymphs. It will do both of you good, and especially Bessian."

And now they were heading towards the grim Northern Plateau. This *Rrafsh*, about which she had read and heard so much during her studies at the institute for young ladies named "The Queen Mother," and especially later during her engagement to Bessian, attracted her and alarmed her at the same time. In fact, what she had read and heard on the subject, and even Bessian's own writings had not given her any idea of what life was really like up there in the highlands amidst the never-ending mists. It seemed to her that everything people said about the High Plateau took on at once an ambiguous, nebulous character. Bessian Vorpsi had written half-tragic, half-philosophical sketches about the North, to which the press had responded in a rather halfway fashion too: some reviewers had hailed the pieces as jewels of the first water, and others had criticized them as lacking in realism. On a number of occasions it had occurred to Diana that if her husband had decided to undertake this rather strange tour, it was not so much to show her what was so remarkable about the North as to settle something that he felt within him. But each time she had given up the idea, thinking that if that was his object he could have taken that trip long ago, and alone at that.

She was watching him now, and from the way his set jaw made his cheekbones more prominent, and the way he stared through the carriage windows, she felt that he was holding back his impatience—which she found quite understandable. He was certainly telling himself that this part-imaginary, part-epic world that he talked about for days on end was taking its time about showing itself. Outside, on either side of the carriage, the endless wasteland unfolded, without a sign of human presence, its countless grey rocks watered by the dullest downpour in the world. He's afraid that I'll be disappointed, she thought, and several times she was on the point of saying, "Don't worry, Bessian, we've only been travelling an hour, and I'm not so impatient or so naive as to think that all the wonders of the North are going to appear before

64

our eyes at once." But she did not say those words; unselfconsciously, she rested her head on his shoulder. She knew that the gesture was more reassuring than any words, and she stayed a long time like that, looking out of the corner of her eye at her light chestnut hair moving upon his shoulder with the motion of the carriage.

She was nearly asleep when she felt his shoulder move.

"Diana, look," he said softly, taking her hand.

In the distance, beside the road, there were some black figures.

"Mountain people?" she asked.

"Yes."

As their carriage drew nearer, the dark figures seemed to grow taller. Both the passengers' faces were glued to the window, and Diana several times wiped from the glass the mist made by their breath.

"What are they holding in their hands, umbrellas?" she asked, but very softly, when the carriage was no more than fifty paces from the mountaineers.

"Yes, that's what it looks like," he muttered. "Where did they get those umbrellas?"

At last the carriage passed the mountaineers, who stared after it. Bessian turned his head, as if to make sure that the things they had in their hands really were old umbrellas with broken struts and ragged cloth.

"I've never seen mountaineers carrying brollies," he murmured. Diana was surprised too, but she took care not to mention it, so as not to make him angry.

When further on they saw another group of mountaineers, two of whom were laden with sacks, Diana pretended not to see them. Bessian looked at them for a while.

"Corn," he said at last, but Diana did not answer. Again

she leaned her head upon his shoulder, and again her hair began to slide gently to and fro with the movement of the carriage.

Now it was he who watched the road attentively. As for her, she tried to turn her thoughts to more pleasant things. After all, it was no great misfortune if a legendary mountaineer heaved a sack of corn onto his back, or carried a dilapidated umbrella against the rain. Had she not seen more than one man from the mountains, in the city streets at the end of autumn, with an axe over his shoulder, and crying out plaintively, "Any wood to cut?", a cry that was more like the cry of a night bird. But Bessian had told her that those people were not representative of the mountain country. Having left, for various reasons, the homeland of epic, they were uprooted like trees overthrown, they had lost their heroic character and deep-seated virtue. The real mountaineers are up there, on the *Rrafsh,* he had said to her one night, lifting his arms towards the celestial heights beyond the horizon, as if the *Rrafsh* were somewhere in the sky rather than on earth.

Now, pressed against the window, he never turned his eyes from the desolate landscape, for fear that his wife might ask: these poor wayfarers, with their skeletal umbrellas in hand, or their backs bent under a sack of corn, are these the legendary mountain stalwarts of whom you have told me so much? But Diana, even if she were to lose all her illusions, would never ask him that question.

Leaning against him, her eyes closing now and then with the jolting of the carriage, as if to ward off the sadness that the barren scene aroused in her, she thought in a fragmentary way about the days when they were first acquainted and the early weeks of their engagement. The chestnut trees lining the boulevard, café doors, the glitter of rings as they embraced, park benches strewn with autumn leaves, and dozens of other such memories—all those things she poured out upon the endless waste, in the hope that those images might in some sort people the void. But the wasteland did not change. Its wet nakedness was ready to engulf in a moment not just her own store of happiness but perhaps the heaped-up joy of whole generations. She herself had never seen such a country. The mountains that loomed above her were well named "the Accursed Mountains."

She was pulled out of her dozing state by a movement of his shoulder, and then by his voice, which had a tender note.

"Diana, look. A church."

She drew near the glass pane and caught sight of the cross that surmounted the stone belfry. The church rose up from a rocky height, and since the road descended very steeply, or perhaps because of the grey background of the sky, the black cross seemed to rise up and sway threateningly among the clouds. The church was still far off, but as they drew closer, they could make out the bell and its bronze shimmer spreading abroad like a smile beneath that black cross-shaped menace.

"How beautiful!" Diana exclaimed.

Bessian nodded, but did not speak. The dark shadow of the cross and the pleasant gleam of the bell soared aloft in every direction and must have been visible, one and inseparable, for miles around.

"Oh, look. There are the *kullas* of the mountains," he said.

With difficulty, she turned her eyes from the church to look for the high stone dwellings.

"Where are they?"

"Look up there on that slope," he said, pointing. "And there, there's another farther on, on that other hill."

"Ah, yes!"

Suddenly he came to life, and his eyes began to search the horizon avidly.

"Mountaineers," he said, his hand stretched out towards the little window in front.

The mountaineers were coming towards them, but they were still a long way off and you could hardly see them.

"There must be a big village somewhere near."

The carriage drew nearer to them, and Diana guessed at her husband's sense of strain.

"They have rifles slung on their shoulders," she said.

"Yes," he said, relieved, not taking his eyes from the window. He was looking for something else. The mountaineers were now no more than twenty paces away.

"There," he called out at last, seizing Diana by the shoulder. "You see the black ribbon on his right sleeve. Do you see?"

"Yes, yes," she said.

"There's another mark of death. And there's another."

Excitement made his breathing irregular.

"How terrible!" The words had escaped her.

"What?"

"I meant to say that it's beautiful and terrible at the same time."

"Yes, it's true. It's tragically beautiful, or wonderfully tragic, if you will."

He turned towards her, suddenly, with an odd light in his eye, as if to say: Admit it. You never believed all this. As it happened, she had never mentioned any such doubt.

The carriage had left the mountaineers behind, and Bessian, his face lit with a smile now, had thrown himself back in his seat.

"We are entering the shadow-land," he said, as if talking to himself, "the place where the laws of death prevail over the laws of life."

"But how does one tell the difference between those whose duty it is to avenge a killing and those from whom vengeance is sought?" she asked. "The black ribbon is the same for everyone, isn't it?"

"Yes, it's the same. The mark of death is exactly the same for those who mean to kill and those who are being hunted."

"How horrible," she said.

"In no other country in the world can one see people on the road who bear the mark of death, like trees marked for felling."

She looked at him kindly. Bessian's eyes shone with the deep brilliance that bursts out after unbearable waiting. Now, those other mountain folk, with their ridiculous ramshackle umbrellas, their prosaic sacks of corn on their backs, seemed never to have been.

"Look, there are still some more of them," he said.

This time she was the one who first saw the black ribbon on the sleeve of one among them.

"Yes, now I can say that we are well within death's kingdom," Bessian said, never turning his eyes from the window. Outside, the rain was still falling, a fine rain, as if diluted with mist.

Diana started to smile.

"Yes," he said, "we have entered death's kingdom like Ulysses, with this difference—Ulysses had to descend in order to reach it, but we must climb."

She listened, looking at him still. He had leaned his forehead against the glass that was clouded over by their breath. Beyond it, the world seemed transformed.

"They wander these roads with that black ribbon on their sleeves like ghosts in the mist," he said.

She listened, but she did not speak. How many times, before they had started out, had he talked about these things, but now his words had a different sound. Behind them, like a film scene behind the subtitles, the landscape looked even more somber. She wanted to ask him if they would also meet on the roads men whose heads were muffled up in their shrouds, whom he had mentioned once, but something kept her from asking. Perhaps it was simply fear that just asking the question would provoke the apparition.

The carriage had gone quite some distance now, and the village was out of sight. Only the cross above the church swayed slowly on the horizon, leaning to one side like crosses on graves, as if the sky, imitating the soil in cemeteries, had also fallen in a little.

"There's a cairn," he said, pointing to the roadside.

She leaned forward to see better. It was a heap of stones somewhat lighter in color than those around the spot, piled carelessly with no obvious design. She thought that if it had not rained that day, those stones would not look so forlorn. She told him that, but he smiled and shook his head.

"The _muranë_, as they are called, always look sad," he said. "More than that, the more pleasant the countryside the sadder they look."

"That may be so," she replied.

"I've seen all kinds of tombs and graveyards, with every

sort of sign and symbol," he went on, "but I don't think there is any grave more real than the simple heap our mountain people build, on the very spot where a man was killed."

"That's true," she said. "It has an air of tragedy about it."

"And the very word, *muranë*, naked, cruel, suggesting pain that nothing can soften—isn't that so?"

She nodded and sighed again. Roused by his own words, he went on talking. He spoke of the absurdity of life, and the reality of death in the North country, about the men of those parts who were esteemed or despised essentially in terms of the relations they created with death, and he brought up the terrible wish expressed by the mountaineers on the birth of a child. "May he have a long life, and die by the rifle!" Death by natural causes, from illness or from old age, was shameful to the man of the mountain regions, and the only goal of the mountaineer during his entire life was laying up the hoard of honor that would allow him to expect a modest memorial on his death.

"I've heard certain songs about the men who are killed," she said. "They are just like their graves, their *muranë*."

"That's true. They weigh on the heart like a heap of stones. In fact, the same concept that governs the structure of the *muranë* governs the structure of the songs."

Diana barely repressed another sigh. Minute by minute, she felt as if something were collapsing inside her. As if he guessed what she felt, he hastened to tell her that if all this was very sad, at the same time it had grandeur. He set himself to explaining to her that, when all was said and done, the aspect of death conferred on the lives of these men something of the eternal, because its very grandeur

71

raised them above paltry things and the petty meanness of life.

"To measure one's days by the yardstick of death, isn't that a very special gift?"

She smiled, shrugging her shoulders.

"That is what the Code does," Bessian went on, "particularly in the section devoted to the law of the blood feud. Do you remember?"

"Yes," she said, "I remember quite well."

"It is a genuine constitution of death," he said, turning suddenly towards her. "People tell a lot of stories about it, and yet, however wild and merciless it may be, I'm convinced of one thing, that it is one of the most monumental constitutions that have come into being in the world, and we Albanians ought to be proud of having begotten it."

He seemed to wait for a word of approval, but she was silent; her eyes, however, looked into his with the same kindness.

"Yes, it's only fair, we should be proud of it," he went on. "The *Rrafsh* is the only region of Europe which— while being an integral part of a modern state, an integral part, I repeat, of a modern European state and not the habitat of primitive tribes—has rejected the laws, the legal institutions, the police, the courts, in short, all the structures of the state; which has rejected these things, you understand, because at one time it was subject to them, and it has renounced them, replacing them with other moral rules which are themselves just as adequate, so much so as to constrain the administrations set up by foreign occupying powers, and later the administration of the independent Albanian state, forcing them to recognize those rules, and thus to put the High Plateau, let's say

72

nearly half of the kingdom, quite beyond the control of the state."

Diana's eyes sometimes followed the movements of her husband's lips, sometimes his eyes.

"That history is very old," he continued. "It began to crystallize when the Constantine of the ballad rose from the grave to keep his pledged word. Did you ever think, when we were studying that ballad in school, that the *bessa* mentioned in it is one of the foundation stones of a structure as majestic as it is terrifying? Because the *Kanun* is not merely a constitution," he went on fervently, "it is also a colossal myth that has taken on the form of a constitution. Universal riches compared to which the Code of Hammurabi and the other legal structures of those regions look like children's toys. Do you follow me? That is why it is foolish to ask, like children, if it is good or bad. Like all great things, the *Kanun* is beyond good and evil. It is beyond. . . . "

At those words she was offended and her cheeks burned. A month ago she herself had put that very question to him: Is the Code good or bad? Then he had smiled without answering her, but now. . . .

"You needn't be sarcastic!" She withdrew to the far end of the seat.

"What?"

It took some minutes before they came to an understanding. He laughed aloud, swore to her that he had never meant to offend her, that he did not even remember that she had once put the question to him, and he ended by asking her to forgive him.

That little incident seemed to bring a bit of life into the carriage. They embraced, they caressed each other, then

73

she opened her handbag and took out her pocket mirror to see if the light lipstick had rubbed away. That little business was accompanied by lively talk about their friends and about Tirana, which, it suddenly seemed to her, they had left long ago, and when they spoke again about the Code, the conversation was no longer stiff and cold, like the edge of an old sword, but more natural, perhaps because they mentioned especially those parts of the Code that dealt with daily life. When just before their engagement, he had given her as a present a fine edition of the *Kanun*, she had read those very passages without paying much attention, and she had forgotten most of the prescriptions that he was citing to her now.

From time to time, they returned in spirit to the streets of the capital and spoke of friends they knew, but it was enough for a mill, a flock of sheep, or a lone traveller to appear on the horizon, for Bessian to bring up the articles of the Code that dealt with those things.

"The *Kanun* is universal," he said at one point. "It has not forgotten a single aspect of economics or ethics."

A little before midday they came upon a wedding party, a cavalcade of *krushks*, and he explained to her that the order of the guests conformed to very strict rules, any breach of which could turn the wedding into a funeral. "Oh, look, there, at the end of the cavalcade, the chief of the *krushks,* the *krushkapar*, the bride's father or brother, leading a horse by the bridle."

Diana, her face pressed to the window, delighted, could not take her eyes from the costumes of the women. How beautiful, Lord, how beautiful, she repeated to herself, while, leaning against her he recited in a caressing voice the clauses of the Code dealing with the *krushks*: "The wedding day can never be put off to another time. In the

74

case of a death in the family, the *krushks* will go to meet the bride nonetheless. The bride enters on one side, the dead man leaves on the other. On the one side people weep, on the other side they sing."

When they had left the wedding party behind them, they talked about the notorious "blessed cartridge" that, in accordance with the Code, the bride's family gave to the groom so that he could use it to shoot his wife if she proved unfaithful, even telling him, "May your hand be blessed," and the two, joking about what would happen if she or he were to violate their marriage vows, they teased each other, and pulled their ears as a sign of reproach, saying, "May your hand be blessed!"

"You are a child," said Bessian, when the storm of laughter had passed, and she felt that at bottom he hated to joke about the *Kanun*, and that he had done so only to give her that small pleasure.

The Code is never a laughing matter, she remembered someone saying, but at once she dismissed the thought from her mind. She had to look outside the coach two or three times before her fit of laughter passed. The landscape had changed, the sky seemed to have opened out, and just because it seemed enlarged it was even more oppressive. She thought she saw a bird, and almost cried aloud, "A bird!" as if she had found in the sky a sign of forbearance or understanding. But what she had seen was only another cross, leaning slightly, like the first one, in the deeps of fog. Somewhere farther on, she thought, there are Franciscan monasteries, and still farther, nuns' convents.

The carriage drove on with its slight, rhythmic swaying. Sometimes, fighting against sleep, she heard his voice that seemed to come from far off, muffled in a cavernous echo. He went on citing articles of the Code to her, chiefly those having to do with everyday life. He talked to her about the rules of hospitality, in general referring to all the provisions concerning the guest within one's gates, which, for an Albanian was sacred, quite beyond comparison with anything else. "Do you remember the definition of a house in the *Kanun*?" he said. "'An Albanian's house is the dwelling of God and the guest.' Of God and the guest, you see. So before it is the house of its master, it is the house of one's guest. The guest, in an Albanian's life, represents the supreme ethical category, more important than blood relations. One may pardon the man who spills the blood of one's father or of one's son, but never the blood of a guest."

He came back again and again to the laws of hospitality, but even in her drowsy state, she felt that his exposition of those ancient prescriptions, rolling on, grating away like the rusty teeth of a cogwheel, went from the peaceful side of daily life under the Code to the bloody side. No matter how one dealt with the Code, one always ended up there. And now, in a voice dressed in those resonances, he was recounting to her an incident that was typical of the world of the *Kanun*. She kept her eyes closed still, clinging to her half-sleep, for she sensed that only in that way would his voice come to her with those far-off echoes. That voice was telling her about a wayfarer travelling alone in the dark, at the foot of a steep mountain. Knowing that he was being hunted for blood vengeance, he had managed to keep safe from his avenger for a long time. Suddenly, on the highroad, with the night coming on, he was seized by a dark premonition. All around, there was nothing but the open heath, not a house, not a living soul from whom he could claim the protection due to a guest. He could see only a herd of goats that had been left to themselves by the herdsman. Then, so as to help pluck up his courage, or maybe so as not to die and disappear without a trace, he called out to the goatherd three times. No voice answered him. Then he called out to the buck with the big bell, "O buck with the big bell, if anything should happen to me, tell your master that before I reached the crest of the hill I was killed under your *bessa*." And as if he had known what would happen, a few paces further on he was killed by the man who was lying in wait for him.

Diana opened her eyes.

"And then?" she asked, "what happened then?"

Bessian smiled a wry smile.

"Another goatherd who was not far off heard the stranger's last words and told the man whose herd it was. And that man, even though he had never known the victim, had never seen him nor ever heard his name, left his family, his flock, and all his other concerns, to avenge the stranger who was connected with him under the *bessa*, and so plunged into the whirlwind of the blood feud."

"That's terrible," Diana said. "But it's absurd. There is fatality in it."

"That's true. It is at once terrible, absurd, and fatal, like all the really important things."

"Like all the really important things," she repeated, huddling back into her corner. She was cold. She looked abstractedly into the ragged pass between two mountains, as if she hoped to find in that grey notch the answer to an enigma.

"Yes," Bessian said, as if he had divined her unspoken question, "because to an Albanian a guest is a demi-god."

Diana blinked, so that his words would not strike her so crudely. He lowered his tone, and his voice took on its echo as before, sooner than she would have expected.

"I remember having heard once, that, unlike many peoples among whom the mountains were reserved to the gods, our mountaineers, by the very fact that they lived in the mountains themselves, were constrained either to expel the gods or to adapt themselves to them so as to be able to live with them. Do you follow me, Diana? That explains why the world of the *Rrafsh* is half-real, half-imaginary, harking back to the Homeric ages. And it also explains the creation of demigods like the guest."

He was silent for a moment, listening unawares to the sound of the wheels on the rocky road.

"A guest is really a demi-god," he went on after a while, "and the fact that any one at all can suddenly become a guest does not diminish but rather accentuates his divine character. The fact that this divinity is acquired suddenly, in a single night simply by knocking at a door, makes it even more authentic. The moment a humble wayfarer, his pack on his shoulder, knocks at your door and gives himself up to you as your guest, he is instantly transformed into an extraordinary being, an inviolable sovereign, a law-maker, the light of the world. And the suddenness of the transformation is absolutely characteristic of the nature of the divine. Did not the gods of the ancient Greeks make their appearance suddenly and in the most unpredictable manner? That is just the way the guest appears at an Albanian's door. Like all the gods he is an enigma, and he comes directly from the realms of destiny or fate—call it what you will. A knock at the door can bring about the survival or the extinction of whole generations. That is what the guest is to the Albanians of the mountains."

"But that's terrible," she said.

He pretended not to have heard her and simply smiled,

but with the cold smile of someone who intends to skirt what might well be the real subject of discussion.

"That is why an attack on a guest protected by the *bessa* is to an Albanian the worst possible misfortune, something like the end of the world."

She looked out of the window and she thought that it would be hard to find a more suitable setting for a vision of the end of the world than these mountains.

"A few years ago, something took place in these parts that would astonish anyone but these mountain people," said Bessian, and he put his hand on Diana's shoulder. His hand had never felt so heavy to her. "Something really staggering."

Why doesn't he tell it to me? she wondered, after a silence long enough to seem unwonted. And she was really not in a state to know whether or not she cared to hear yet another disturbing story.

"A man was killed," he said, "not from ambush, but right in the marketplace."

Looking at him sidelong, Diana watched the corners of his lips. He told her that the killing had taken place in broad daylight, in the bustle of the marketplace, and the victim's brothers had set out immediately in pursuit of the killer, for these were the first hours after the murder, when the truce had not yet been asked for, and the bloodshed could be avenged at once. The killer managed to elude his pursuers, but meanwhile the dead man's whole clan was up in arms and was seeking him everywhere. Night was falling, and the murderer, who came from another village, did not know the country well. Fearing that he might be discovered, he knocked at the first door he found on his way, and asked that he be granted the *bessa*. The head of the household took the stranger in and agreed to his wish.

"And can you guess what house it was to which he had come for sanctuary?" said Bessian, with his mouth quite close to her neck.

Diana turned her head suddenly, her eyes wide and motionless.

"It was his victim's house," he said.

"I thought as much. And then? What happened then?"

Bessian took a deep breath. He told her that at first on either side no one suspected what had happened. The killer understood that the house to which he had come as a guest had been stricken with misfortune, but he never imagined that he himself had brought it about. The head of the house, on his part, in spite of his grief, welcomed the visitor in keeping with the custom, guessing that he had just killed someone and was being pursued, but not suspecting—he, too—that the murdered man was his own son.

And so they sat together by the hearth, eating and drinking coffee. As for the dead man, in keeping with the custom, he had been laid out in another room.

Diana started to say something, but she felt that the only words she could possibly utter were, "absurd" and "fateful"; she preferred to be silent.

Bessian resumed, "Late in the evening, worn out by the long chase, the brothers of the murdered man came home. As soon as they came in they saw the guest sitting by the hearth, and they recognized him."

Bessian turned his head towards his wife to gauge the effect of his words. "Don't be afraid," he said. "Nothing happened."

"What?"

"Nothing at all. At first, in a fury, the brothers reached

80

for their weapons, but a word from their father was enough to stop them and to calm them. I think you can imagine what it was that he said."

Embarrassed, she shook her head.

"The old man simply said, 'He is a guest. Don't touch him.'"

"And then? What happened then?"

"Then they sat down with their enemy and guest for as long as the custom required. They conversed with him, they prepared a bed for him, and in the morning they escorted him to the village boundary."

Diana pressed two fingers between her eyebrows, as if she meant to extract something from her forehead.

"So that is their conception of a guest."

Bessian brought out that sentence between two silences, as one sets an object in an empty space in order to throw it into relief. He waited for Diana to say "That's terrible," as she had the first time, or to say something else, but she said nothing. She kept her fingers on her forehead, where the brows meet, as if she could not find the thing that she wanted to tear away.

The muffled panting of the horses reached them from outside, and the coachman's occasional whistles. Together with these sounds, Diana heard her husband's voice, which for some reason had again become deep and slow.

"And now," he said, "the question that arises is to understand why the Albanians have created all that."

He talked on, his head quite close to her shoulder, as if he meant to ask her for answers to all the questions or speculations that he advanced, though his delivery scarcely allowed for any responses on her part. He went on to ask (it was not clear if the questions were addressed to himself, or Diana, or someone else), why the Albanians had created the institution of the guest, exalting it above all other human relations, even those of kinship.

"Perhaps the answer lies in the democratic character of this institution," he said, setting himself to think his way through the matter. "Any ordinary man, on any day, can be raised to the lofty station of a guest. The path to that temporary deification is open to anybody at any time. Isn't that so, Diana?"

"Yes," she said softly, without taking her hand from her forehead.

He shifted in his seat, as if looking both for a more comfortable position and for the most appropriate language in which to express his idea.

"Given that anyone at all can grasp the sceptre of the guest," he went on, "and since that sceptre, for every Albanian, surpasses even the king's sceptre, may we not assume that in the Albanian's life of danger and want, that to be a guest if only for four hours or twenty-four hours, is a kind of respite, a moment of oblivion, a truce, a reprieve, and—why not?—an escape from everyday life into some divine reality?"

He fell silent, as if waiting for a reply, and Diana, feeling that she had to say something to him, found it easier to lay her head on his shoulder again.

Bessian found that the familiar odor of his wife's hair rather disturbed the stream of his thoughts. Just as the greening of nature gives us the feeling of spring, or snow the feeling of winter, her chestnut hair tumbling over his shoulder aroused in him better than anything else the sensation of happiness. The thought that he was a happy man began to shine feebly in his consciousness, and in the velvet jewel-case of the carriage, that idea took on the secret languor of luxurious things.

"Are you tired?" he asked.

"Yes, a bit."

He slipped his arm around her shoulders and drew her gently to him, breathing in the perfume of his young wife's body, given off subtly, like every valued thing.

"We'll be there soon."

Without removing his arm, he lowered his head slightly towards the window so as to glance outside.

"In an hour, an hour and a half at most, we'll be there," he said.

Through the glass, one could see in the distance, standing out clearly, the jagged outlines of the mountains in that March afternoon flooded with rain.

"What district are we in?"

He looked outside but did not answer her, merely shrugging his shoulders to indicate that he did not know. She remembered the days before their departure (days that now seemed to have been torn away not from this month of March, but from another March, as far off as the stars), filled with witty sayings, with laughter, with jokes, fears, jealousies, all stemming from their "northern adventure" as Adrian Guma had dubbed it when they had met him at the post office where they were composing a telegram to send to someone who lived on the High Plateau. He had said, That's like sending a message to the birds or to the thunderbolts. Then the three had laughed, and in all the merriment, Adrian had gone on asking, "You really have an address up there? Forgive me, I just can't believe it."

"A little while longer and we'll be there," Bessian said for the third time, leaning towards the window. Diana wondered how he could know that they were approaching their destination, travelling on a road without signposts or milestones. As for Bessian, he was thinking that he did not have time to say more about the cult of hospitality, just as evening was drawing on, and they were drawing nearer and nearer to the tower in which they would spend the night.

"In a little while, this evening, we shall assume the crown of the guest," he murmured, only just touching her cheek with his lips. She moved her head towards him, her breath came faster as in their most intimate moments, but it ended in a sigh.

"What's the matter?"

"Nothing," she said quietly. "I'm just a little frightened."

"Really?" he said, laughing. "But how can that be?"

"I don't know."

He shook his head for a moment, as if her half-smile, close to his face, were the flicker of a match that he must try to blow out.

"Well, Diana, let me tell you that it doesn't matter at all that we are in death's kingdom—you can be sure that you have never been so well shielded from danger or the least affront. No royal pair has ever had more devoted guards ready to sacrifice their present and their future than we shall have tonight. Doesn't that give you a sense of security?"

"That's not what I was thinking about," Diana said, changing her position on the seat. "I'm troubled by something else, and I don't really know how to explain it. A little while ago you talked about divinity, destiny, fatality. They are all very fine things, but they are frightening, too. I don't want to bring misfortune to anyone."

84

"Oh," he said gaily, "like every sovereign, you find the crown both alluring and frightening. That's quite understandable, since, after all, if every crown is glorious, every crown is woeful, too."

"That's enough, Bessian," she said quietly. "Don't make fun of me."

"I'm not making fun of you," he said with the same playful air. "I have the very same feeling. The guest, the *bessa*, and vengeance are like the machinery of classical tragedy, and once you are caught up in the mechanism, you must face the possibility of tragedy. But despite all that, Diana, we have nothing to fear. In the morning, we'll take off our crowns and be relieved of their weight until the night."

He felt her fingers stroking his neck, and he pressed his head against her hair. How shall we sleep there, she wondered, together or apart? And now she asked him aloud, "Is it still very far?"

Bessian opened the carriage door a little to put the question to the coachman, whose existence he had nearly forgotten. The man's reply was accompanied by a blast of cold air.

"We're nearby," he said.

"Brr, it's cold," Diana said.

Outside, the afternoon that until then had seemed never-ending, showed the first signs of fading. The panting of the horses now became louder, and Diana imagined the froth of foam at their mouths as they drew the carriage towards the unknown *kulla* where Bessian and herself were to stay the night.

Dusk had not quite fallen when the carriage halted. The couple got down. After the long clop-clapping of hooves, the protracted jolting, the world seemed mute and frozen.

The coachman pointed to one of the towers that rose up a good distance away beside the road, but Bessian and Diana, whose legs were quite stiff, wondered how they would manage to reach it.

For a while they prowled about the coach, climbing in again to take their travelling bags and suitcases, and they set out at last towards the tower—an odd procession, the couple, arm in arm, leading the way, followed by the coachman who was carrying their suitcases.

When they drew near the tower, Bessian let go his wife's arm, and with steps that she thought not very confident, went right up to the stone building. The narrow door was closed, and there was no sign of life at the loopholes, and in a flash a question came to him: Had they received their telegram?

Now Bessian halted before the *kulla*, and he looked up to call out, according to custom, "O, master of the house, are you receiving guests?" In other circumstances, Diana would have burst out laughing to see her husband playing the part of a visiting mountaineer, but now something restrained her. Perhaps it was the shadow of the tower (stone casts a heavy shadow, the old men said) that was putting a weight on her heart.

Bessian raised his head a second time, and to Diana who was looking at him, he seemed small and defenseless at the foot of that cold, thousand-year-old wall to which he was about to call out.

Midnight had long passed, but Diana, who was alternately too cold and too hot under two heavy woollen blankets, had not managed to go to sleep. They had arranged a bed for her on the second storey, right on the floor with the women and girls of the household. Bessian had been installed on the storey above, in the guest chamber. He too, she thought, could not possibly have fallen asleep.

From beneath her came the lowing of an ox. At first she was terrified, but one of the women of the house who was lying beside her, said in a low voice, "Don't be frightened, it's Kazil." Diana remembered that animals that chew the cud make that sort of noise when digesting, and she felt reassured. But nevertheless she still could not go to sleep.

Her mind was full of scraps of notions and opinions that came to her confusedly and with no particular emphasis, things heard long ago or a few hours before. She thought that her not being able to sleep came from that very confusion, and she tried to put those things in some kind of order. But it was a difficult task. As soon as she managed to channel one line of thought, another revolted at once, spilling out of its bed. For a while she tried to concentrate on the rest of their trip, as Bessian and she had planned it before their departure. She began to count the days they were to spend in the mountains, the houses that they were to stay in, some of which were quite unknown to her, like the *Kulla* of Orosh, where they were going to be received the next day by the mysterious lord of the *Rrafsh*. Diana tried to imagine all that, but at that very moment her mind wandered. She put her hands to her temples, as if to slow the rapid beating that seemed to come from the excitation of her brain, but in a little while she felt that the pressure seemed to make the giddy sensation worse. So she removed her hands, and for a moment she let her thoughts wander as they would. But that became intolerable. I must think of something ordinary, she said to herself. And she began to call up what they had talked about a few hours earlier in the guest chamber. I'm going to bring it all to mind again, she thought, like the ox in the stall down there. Bessian would certainly appreciate the image. He had been very attentive to her in the guest chamber a while ago. He had explained everything to her, first asking permission of the master of the house. For in the guest chamber, or the men's chamber, as it was also called, no whispering or private conversation was allowed. All the talk there as Bessian explained to her was on men's concerns, gossip was forbidden, as were incomplete sentences or half-formed thoughts, and every remark was greeted with the words, "You have spoken well," or "May your mouth be blessed." "There, listen to what they are saying," Bessian had whispered. And she found that the conversation did in fact proceed in just the way he had told her it would. Given the fact that an Albanian's home is a fortress in the literal sense of the word, Bessian told her, and since the structure of the family, according to the Code, resembles a little state, it is understandable that an Albanian's conversation will more or less reflect those conditions in its style. Then, in the course of the evening, Bessian had come back to his favorite subject, the guest and hospitality, and had explained to her that the concept of "the guest," like every great idea, carried with it not only its sublime aspect but its absurd aspect too. "Here, this evening, we are invested with the power of the gods," he said. "We can abandon ourselves to any kind of madness, even commit a murder—and it is the master of the house who will bear the responsibility for it, because he has welcomed us to his table. Hospitality has its duties, says the *Kanun*, but there are limits that even we, the gods, may not transgress. And do you know what those limits are? If, as I have said, everything is possible for us, there is one thing that is forbidden, and that is to lift the lid of the pot on the fire." Diana could hardly keep from laughing. "But that's ridiculous," she muttered. "Perhaps," he said, "But it's true. If I were to do that tonight, the master of the house would rise at once, go to the window, and with a terrible cry, proclaim to the village that his table had been insulted by a guest. And at that very moment the guest becomes a deadly enemy." "But why?" Diana asked. "Why must it be that way?" Bessian shrugged his shoulders. "I don't know," he said. "I don't know how to explain it. Perhaps it's in the logic of things that every great idea has a flaw that does not diminish it but brings it more within our reach." While he spoke, she looked about surreptitiously, and several times she was on the point of saying, "Yes, it's true, these things have a certain grandeur, but might there not be a little more cleanliness here? After all, if a woman can be compared with a mountain nymph, she must have a *salle de bain*." But Diana had said nothing, not at all because she did not have the courage, but so as not to lose the thread of her thought. To tell the truth, this was one of the few cases in which she had not told him just what she was thinking. Usually, she let him know whatever thoughts happened to come to her, and indeed he never took it amiss if she let slip a word that might pain him, because when all was said and done that was the price one paid for sincerity.

Diana turned the other way on her bed, perhaps for the hundredth time. Her thoughts had begun to get mixed up in her mind while she and Bessian were still in the guest room. Despite her efforts to listen with attention to everything that was said, in that room her mind had started leaping from bough to bough. Now, as she listened to the noises of the cattle below (she smiled to herself once again) she began to feel the fearful approach of sleep put to flight at once by the creaking of a floorboard or by a sudden cramp. At one point she groaned, "Why did you bring me here?" and was surprised by her own cry, because she was still awake enough to hear her voice but she could not make out the words. And now sleep spread before her imagination, looking like the wilderness that they had travelled through, strewn everywhere with pots whose covers must never be removed, and then she performed the forbidden act, reaching out her hand towards them—which was causing all that plaintive creaking.

This is torture, she thought, and she opened her eyes. Before her, on the dark wall, she could see a patch of dim light. For a long moment, as if spellbound, she stared at the greyish patch. Where had it been, why hadn't she noticed it sooner? Outdoors, as it seemed, day was breaking. Diana could not take her eyes from that narrow window. In the depressing darkness of the room, that shred of dawn was like a message of salvation. Diana felt its soothing effect freeing her swiftly from her terrors. Many mornings must have been condensed in that bit of grey light; if not it could never have been so alert, so tranquil, and so indifferent to the terrors of the night. Under its influence, Diana fell asleep quickly.

The carriage was travelling again over a mountain road. The day was grey, and the dull horizon closed down upon the distant heights. The men who had escorted Diana and Bessian had turned back, and the two were alone again, uncrowned guests, showing signs of fatigue from the past night, seated on the velvet-covered bench.

"Did you sleep well?" he asked her.

"Not much. Just towards morning."

"Me too. I scarcely closed my eyes."

"I thought as much."

Bessian took her hand and held it. It was the first time since their marriage that they had slept apart. He glanced at her profile out of the corner of his eye. She seemed pale to him. He wanted to kiss her, but something that he did not understand held him back.

For a while he kept his eyes on the small carriage window, and then, without turning his head, he looked furtively at his wife once again. Her pale face seemed cold to him. Her hand lay inertly in his. He asked her, "What's the matter?" but in fact no word came out. A faint alarm sounded somewhere deep within him.

Perhaps it was not really coldness? It was rather a certain detachment, or the first stage of a kind of estrangement from him.

The carriage rolled along, shaking more or less rhythmically, and he told himself that perhaps it was neither one nor the other. No, certainly not, he thought, neither one nor the other. It was something more simple: taking up the proper distance, that ability to slough one's skin and become a far-off star which every human being has, and was really one of the reasons for her withdrawing. That was what had been emphasized this morning in Diana's case, and what had particularly struck him, accustomed as he was to feeling her very close to him and very understanding.

The grey daylight found its way only sparingly into the carriage, and in addition the velvet upholstery absorbed part of it, deepening the gloom: Bessian thought that he might be in the early stage of a coming defeat, at the moment when one cannot tell if the savor is pleasant or bitter—for he thought himself sufficiently acute to see defeat where others would still see victory.

He smiled to himself and realized that he was not in the least unhappy. After all, she had always found him somewhat remote, and there was no harm if she were to become a little aloof herself. Perhaps she would seem even more desirable to him.

Bessian was surprised that he fetched a deep breath. Other days would come to them in their life together; by turns one would be a riddle to the other, and certainly he would recover the lost ground.

Lord, what ground have I lost that I must recover? He laughed at himself, but his laughter did not show in any part of his body, and it rolled along hollowly within him. And, to persuade himself that his doubts were foolish, once again he looked secretly at his wife's face in the hope that they would be weakened. But Diana's handsome features offered him no reassurance.

They had been travelling for some hours when their carriage halted at the side of the road. Before they had had time to ask why they had stopped, they saw the coachman come up to the window on Bessian's side and open the door. He said that this was a place where they might have lunch.

Only then did Bessian and Diana notice that they had stopped in front of a steep-roofed building that must be an inn.

"Still another four or five hours to the Castle of Orosh," the coachman explained to Bessian. "And I think that there is no other suitable place for refreshment between. Then, the horses need a rest, too."

Without answering, Bessian stepped down and stretched out his hand to his wife to help her. She stepped

92

OTTAKAR'S
a love for books

57 George Street
Edinburgh
EH2 2JQ
Tel: 0131 225 4495
Fax: 0131 225 9626

SALE
27   3 46069   03 Jan 2004 11:53

CASHIER: BILL
9780099449874 Broken April   6.99

	ITEMS	
TOTAL	1	6.99

CASH   20.00
CHANGE CASH   13.01-

Head Office: St John's House,
72 St John's Road, London, SW11 1PT

Vat No: 561997200
Company Reg No: 2133199

down nimbly, and still holding her husband's hand she looked towards the inn. Several people had come to the threshold and were staring at the new arrivals. Another man, the last to emerge from the inn door, approached them with a halting step.

"What can we do for you?" he said respectfully.

It was clear that this man was the innkeeper. The coachman asked him whether they could eat lunch at the inn and whether there was fodder for the horses.

"Certainly. Do come in, please," the man replied, pointing to the door, but looking at a different part of the wall where there was no door nor any kind of entrance. "Enter, and welcome."

Diana looked at him astonished, but Bessian whispered, "he's squint-eyed."

"I have a private room," he explained. "It so happens that the table is taken today, but I'll arrange another one for you. Ali Binak and his assistants have been here for three days," he added proudly. "What did you say? Yes, Ali Binak himself. Don't you know who he is?"

Bessian shrugged.

"Are you from Shkoder? No? From Tirana? Oh, of course, with a carriage like that. Will you stay the night here?"

"No, we're going to the *Kulla* of Orosh."

"Oh, yes. I thought as much. It's more than two years since I saw a carriage like that. Relatives of the prince?"

"No, his guests."

As they passed through the great hall of the inn on the way to their private room, Diana felt the stares of the customers, of whom some were eating lunch at a long, grubby oak table, while others sat in the corners on their packs of thick black woolen cloth. Two or three, sitting on the bare floor, moved a little to let the small group through.

"These past three days we have had a good deal of excitement because of a boundary dispute that is to be settled nearby."

"A boundary dispute?" Bessian asked.

"Yes, sir," said the innkeeper, pushing open a dilapidated door with one hand. "That's why Ali Binak and his assistants have come."

He said these last words in a low voice, just as the travellers crossed the threshold of the private room.

"There they are," whispered the innkeeper, nodding towards an empty corner of the room. But his guests, now used to the innkeeper's squint, looked in another direction, where at an oak table, but smaller and somewhat cleaner than the one in the public room, three men were eating lunch.

"I'll bring another table right away," the innkeeper said, and he disappeared. Two of the diners looked up at the newcomers, but the third went on eating without lifting his eyes from his plate. From behind the door, there came a grating noise punctuated by thumping sounds, drawing nearer and nearer. Soon they saw two table legs, then part of the innkeeper's body, and then the whole table and the innkeeper grotesquely entangled.

He set down the table and left to fetch their seats.

"Please be seated," he said, arranging the stools. "What would you like?"

After asking what there was, Bessian said at last that they would have two fried eggs and some cheese. The innkeeper said, "At your service" to everything, and for a while he was busy coming and going in all directions, trying to serve the new guests without neglecting the earlier ones. While hurrying from one group of his distinguished guests to the other, he seemed to be at a loss, obviously unable to make up his mind which was the more important. It looked as if his uncertainty worsened his physical handicap, and it seemed that he wanted to direct some of his limbs towards one group and some towards the other.

"I wonder just who they think we are," Diana said.

Without raising his head, Bessian glanced sidelong at the three men who were eating lunch. It was apparent that the innkeeper, while bending down to wipe the table with a rag, was telling them about the new arrivals. One of them, the shortest, seemed to be making as if he were not listening, or perhaps he was in fact not listening. The second, who had colorless eyes that seemed to go with his slack, indifferent face, was looking on as if bewildered. The third man, wearing a checked jacket, could not keep his eyes off Diana. He was obviously drunk.

"Where is the place where the boundaries are to be established?" Bessian asked when the innkeeper served Diana her fried eggs.

"At Wolf's Pass, sir," the landlord said. "It is a half-hour's walk from here. But if you go by carriage, of course, it will take less time."

"What do you say, Diana, shall we go? It should be interesting."

"If you like," she said.

"Has there been feuding over the boundaries, or killings?" Bessian asked the innkeeper.

The man whistled. "Certainly, sir. That's a strip of land greedy for death, studded with *muranës* time out of mind."

"We'll go without fail," Bessian said.

"If you like," his wife said again.

"This is the third time that they have called on Ali Binak, and still the dispute and the blood-letting have not ended," the landlord said.

At that moment the short man got up from the table. From the way the other two rose immediately after him, Bessian surmised that he must be Ali Binak.

That man nodded towards them, without looking at anyone in particular, and led the way out. The two others followed. The man in the checked jacket brought up the rear, still devouring Diana with his reddened eyes.

"What a revolting man," Diana said.

Bessian gestured vaguely.

"You mustn't cast the first stone. Who knows how long he's been wandering through these mountains, without a wife, without pleasure of any kind. Judging by his clothes, he must be a city man."

"Even so, he might spare me those oily looks," Diana said, pushing away her plate; She had eaten only one egg.

Bessian called the innkeeper for the bill.

"If the gentleman and the lady want to go to Wolf's Pass, Ali Binak and his assistants have just started out. You could follow them in your carriage. Or perhaps you need someone to accompany you. . . . "

"We'll follow their horses," Bessian said.

The coachman was drinking coffee in the public room. He rose at once and followed them. Bessian looked at his watch.

"We have a good two hours in which to see a boundary settlement, haven't we?"

The coachman shook his head doubtfully.

"I don't know what to say, sir. From here to Orosh is a long way. However, if that's what you want to do. . . . "

"We'll be all right if we reach Orosh before nightfall," Bessian continued. "It's still early afternoon, and we have time. And then, it's an opportunity not to be missed," he added, turning to Diana, who was standing beside him.

She had turned up the fur collar of her coat and was waiting for them to make up their minds.

Ten minutes later, their carriage overtook the horses of Ali Binak's small party. They stood to one side to let the carriage pass, and it took a while for the coachman to explain to them that he did not know the way to Wolf's Pass, and that the carriage would follow after them. Diana was ensconced in the depths of the coach so as to avoid the annoying looks of the man in the checked jacket, whose horse kept appearing on one or the other side of the vehicle.

Wolf's Pass turned out to be farther away than the innkeeper had said. In the distance they saw a bare plain on which some people appeared as moving black specks. As they drew nearer, Bessian tried to recall what the *Kanun* said about boundaries. Diana listened calmly. Bessian said, "Boundary marks shall not be disturbed, any more than the bones of the dead in their graves. Whosoever instigates a murder in a boundary dispute shall be shot by the whole village."

"Are we going to be present at an execution?" Diana asked plaintively. "That's all we needed."

Bessian smiled.

"Don't worry. This must be a peaceful settlement, sin they've invited that—what's his name again? Oh, yes, Binak."

"He seems to me to be a very responsible man," I said. "I wouldn't say as much for one of his assistar man in the clown's jacket—he's repulsive."

"Don't pay any attention to him."

Bessian looked straight ahead, impatient as it seemed, to reach the plain as swiftly as possible.

"Setting up a boundary stone is a solemn act," he said, still staring into the distance. "I don't know if we'll have the good fortune to be present at just such a ceremony. Oh, look. There's a *muranë*.

"Where?"

"There, behind that bush, on the right."

"Oh, yes," Diana said.

"There's another."

"Yes, yes, I see it, and there's another one further on."

"Those are the *muranës* that the innkeeper mentioned," Bessian said. "They serve as boundary marks between fields or property lines."

"There's another," Diana said.

"That's what the *Kanun* says. 'When a death occurs during a boundary dispute, the grave itself serves as a boundary mark.'"

Diana's head was right against the window-pane.

"The tomb that becomes a boundary mark cannot, according to the *Kanun*, ever be displaced by any person to the end of time," Bessian continued. "It is a boundary that has been consecrated by bloodshed and death."

"How many opportunities to die!" Diana said those words against the window-pane, which promptly steamed over, as if to cut her off from the sight of the landscape.

In front of them the three horsemen were dismounting. The carriage halted a few paces behind. As soon as Bessian and Diana stepped down from the coach, they felt that everyone's attention was directed at themselves. Assembled all around them were men, women, and many children.

"There are children here, too, do you see?" Bessian said to Diana. "Establishing the boundaries is the only important event in the life of a mountaineer to which the children come, and that is done so as to preserve the memory of it for as long as possible."

They went on talking to each other, supposing that it would allow them to face the curiosity of the mountain people in the most natural-seeming way. Out of the corner of her eye, Diana looked at the young women, the hems of whose long skirts billowed with their every movement. All of them had their hair dyed black and cut in the same style, with curls on their foreheads and straight hair hanging down on each side of their faces like curtains in the theatre. They looked at the newly arrived couple from a distance, but taking care to conceal their interest.

"Are you cold?" Bessian asked his wife.

"A bit."

In fact it was quite cold on the high plateau, and the blue tints of the mountains all around seemed to make the air even colder.

"Lucky it's not raining," Bessian said.

"Why would it be raining?" she said in surprise. For a moment she thought of the rain as being a poor beggar-woman, out of place in this magnificent alpine winter scene.

In the middle of a pasture, Ali Binak and his assistants were carrying on a discussion with a group of men.

"Let's go and see. We're sure to find out something."

They walked on slowly through the scattered people, hearing whispers—the words themselves, partly because they were mumbled and partly because of the unfamiliar dialect, were almost incomprehensible to them. The only words they did understand were "princess" and "the

99

king's sister," and Diana, for the first time that day, wanted to laugh aloud.

"Did you hear?" she said to Bessian. "They take me for a princess."

Happy to see her a little more cheerful, he pressed her arm.

"Not so tired now?"

"No," she said. "It's lovely here."

Without being aware of it, they had been approaching Ali Binak's group. They exchanged introductions almost spontaneously because the mountain people seemed to be pushing the two groups of new arrivals together. Bessian told them who he was and where he came from. Ali Binak did the same, to the astonishment of the mountaineers who believed him to be famous throughout the world. As they talked, the crowd of people around them grew, staring at them and especially at Diana.

"The innkeeper told us a little while ago that this plain has known many disputes about boundaries," Bessian said.

"That is true," Ali Binak replied. He spoke quietly and in a somewhat monotonous tone, with no hint of passion. No doubt that was required of him because of his work as an interpreter of the *Kanun*. "I think you must have seen the *muranës* on either side of the road."

Bessian and Diana both nodded their heads.

"And after all those deaths the dispute is still not settled?" Diana asked.

Ali Binak looked at her calmly. Compared with the curious looks of the crowd around them and especially the blazing eyes of the man with the checked jacket, who had introduced himself as a surveyor, Ali Binak's eyes seemed to Diana to be those of a classical statue.

"No one is quarreling any longer about the boundaries

100

established by bloodshed," he said. "Those have been established forever on the face of the earth. It is the others that still stir up quarrels," and he pointed towards the upland.

"The part that is not bloody?"

"Yes, just so, madam. For a good many years there has been discord over these pastures on the part of two villages, and it has not been brought to an end."

"But is the presence of death indispensable in order for the boundary lines to be lasting?" Diana was surprised at having spoken, and particularly at her tone, in which a certain irony could clearly be distinguished.

Ali Binak smiled coldly.

"We are here, madam, precisely to prevent death from taking a hand in this affair."

Bessian looked at his wife questioningly, as if to say, what has come over you? He thought he saw in her eyes a fleeting light that he had never seen before. Rather hurriedly, as if to wipe away all trace of this small incident, he asked Ali Binak the first question that came to him.

Around them all eyes were trained on the little group that was talking eagerly. Only a few old men sat to one side on some big stones, indifferent to everything.

Ali Binak went on talking slowly and only a minute later did Bessian realize that he had asked about the very thing he should have been careful not to mention, the deaths brought about by boundary disputes.

"If the man doesn't die at once, and he forces himself along, whether walking or crawling, until he reaches someone else's land, then, at the place where he collapses and succumbs to his wounds, there his *muranë* will be built, and even though it is on another's land it remains forever the new boundary mark."

Not only in Ali Binak's appearance but in the syntax of

101

his speech, there was something cold, something alien to ordinary language.

"And what if two men kill each other in the same instant?" Bessian asked.

Ali Binak raised his head. Diana thought she had never seen a man whose authority was so unaffected by his small stature.

"If two men kill each other at a certain distance from each other, then the boundary for each is the place where each man fell, and the space between is reckoned as belonging to no one."

"No-man's land," Diana said. "Exactly as if it were a question of two countries."

"It's just as we were saying yesterday evening," Bessian said. "Not only in their habits of speech, but in thought and action the people of the High Plateau have something of the attributes of independent countries."

"And when there were no rifles?" Bessian went on. "The *Kanun* is older than firearms, isn't it?"

"Yes, older, certainly."

"Then they used blocks of stone for the purpose, didn't they?"

"Yes," said Ali Binak. "Before rifles were available, people practiced trial by ordeal, carrying stones. In the case of a quarrel between two families or villages or banners, each side appointed its champion. He who carried his block of stone farthest was the winner."

"And what will happen today?"

Ali Binak looked around at the scattered crowd and then fixed his eyes upon the small group of old men.

"Venerable elders of this banner have been invited to bear witness about the former boundaries of the pasture."

Bessian and Diana turned towards the old men who

were sitting as if they were actors waiting to be given their roles. They were so ancient that from moment to moment they must certainly have forgotten why they were there.

"Shall you be starting soon?" Bessian said.

Ali Binak took out of his fob a watch fastened by a chain.

"Yes," he said. "I think we shall start very soon."

"Shall we stay?" Bessian asked Diana in a low voice.

"If you like," she replied.

The eyes of the mountain people, particularly of the women and children, followed their every movement, but now Bessian and Diana were somewhat accustomed to it. Diana was anxious only to avoid the tipsy stare of the surveyor. He and the other assistant, who had been introduced at the inn as a doctor, followed Ali Binak step by step, although he seemed to ignore their presence, never speaking to them.

A certain restlessness suggested that the time to begin the ceremony was at hand. Ali Binak and his assistants, who had deserted the visitors, went from one group of people to the next. Only now, after the little crowd had moved, did Bessian and Diana notice the old boundary stones strung out along a line that crossed the plateau from one end to the other.

Suddenly, a feeling of expectancy seemed to invade the country round. Diana slipped her arm under Bessian's and pressed herself against him.

"But what if something happens?" she said.

"What sort of thing?"

"All the mountaineers are armed. Haven't you noticed?"

He stared at her, and he was about to say, when you saw those two mountaineers with their ramshackle umbrellas you thought you could make fun of the High Plateau region, and now you sense the danger, don't you? But he remembered that she had not said a thing about the umbrellas, and that he had concocted all this in his mind.

"You mean that someone might be killed," he said. "I don't think so."

In fact, all the mountaineers were armed, and an atmosphere of chill menace hung over the scene. The sleeves of a number of them bore the black ribbon. Diana moved even closer to her husband.

"It will begin soon," he said, still looking at the old men, who had risen to their feet.

Diana's mind was strangely vacant. By chance as she looked about her, her eye fell on their coach. Drawn up on the edge of the pasture, black, with its rococo turnings and its velvet upholstery like that of a theatre loge, it stood out against the grey background of the mountains, completely foreign to the scene, out of place. She wanted to shake Bessian's arm and tell him, "Look at the carriage," but just at that moment, he whispered, "It's beginning."

One of the old men had left his group and he seemed to be getting ready to fulfill a task.

"Let's move a little closer," Bessian said, drawing her along by her hand. "It looks as if both sides have chosen this old man to mark the boundary."

The old man took a few steps forward, and halted beside a stone and a clod of fresh earth. A heavy silence fell upon the plateau, but perhaps that was only an impression, because the grumbling of the mountain heights drowned the noise of conversation, so that the human element by itself, having given way, had no power to still any sound. And yet everyone had the feeling that silence had fallen.

The old man bent down, grasped the big stone with

both hands, and heaved it up on his shoulder. Then someone set the clod of earth on that same shoulder. His withered face with its many brown patches showed no emotion. Then in that silence, a clear, resonant voice that came from someplace one could not identify, cried out: "Go forward, then, and if you do not go in good faith, may this stone crush you in the life to come!"

For a moment the old man's eyes looked as if they had turned to stone. It seemed impossible that his limbs could make the slightest movement without bringing down the whole framework of his ancient body. Nevertheless, he took a step forward.

"Let's go a little closer," Bessian whispered.

Now they were very nearly in the center of the group of people who were following the old man.

"I hear someone speaking. Who is it?" Diana murmured.

"The old man," Bessian answered in the same low tone. "He is swearing by the stone and the earth he carries on his shoulder, as the *Kanun* requires."

The old man's voice, deep, sepulcral, could scarcely be heard.

"By this stone and by this earth that I bear as a burden, by what I have heard from our forefathers, the old boundaries of the pasture are here and here, and here is where I set the boundaries myself. If I lie, may I carry nothing but stone and mud forever!"

The old man, followed by the same small group of people, moved slowly over the pasture. For the last time one could hear, "If I have not spoken truly, let this stone and this earth weigh me down in this life and the next." And he dropped his load to the ground.

Some of the mountaineers who had been following him

105

started at once to dig at all the places that he had pointed out.

"Look, they're prising out the old markers and setting the new ones in place," Bessian explained to his wife.

They heard the sound of hammer-blows. Someone called out, "Bring the children here so that they may see."

Diana watched the setting of the boundary marks unseeing. Suddenly among the black jackets of the mountaineers she saw those hateful checks coming near, and she grasped her husband's sleeve as if to ask him for help. He looked at her questioningly, but she did not have time to say a word to him, for the surveyor was already before them, smiling in a way that seemed even more drunken than before.

"What a farce," he said, cocking his head towards the mountaineers. "What a tragi-comedy! You're a writer, aren't you? Well, write something about this nonsense, please."

Bessian looked at him sternly, but made no reply.

"Pardon me for having troubled you. Especially you, madam, please."

He bowed somewhat theatrically, and Diana smelled alcohol on his breath.

"What do you want?" she said coldly, without concealing her disgust.

The man made as if to speak, but it appeared that Diana's manner overawed him, for he said nothing. He turned his head towards the mountaineers and stayed that way for a moment, his face set, and still lit with a spiteful half-smile.

"It's enough to make you howl," he muttered. "The art of surveying has never suffered a greater insult."

"What?"

"How can I not be indignant at it? You must understand. Of course that's the way I feel. I'm a surveyor. I've studied that science. I've learned the art of measuring land, of drawing up plans. And despite that I wander on the High Plateau all the year through without being able to practice my profession, because the mountain people do not regard a surveyor as having any skill in these matters. You've seen yourself how they settle disputed boundaries. With stones, with curses, with witches and what not. And my instruments spend years on end packed up in my luggage. I left them down there at the inn, in some corner or other. One day they'll steal them on me, if they haven't already—but I'll steal a march on them before they pinch my things. I'll sell them and drink up the proceeds. Oh, unhappy day! I'm going off now, sir. Ali Binak, my master, is beckoning me. Excuse my troubling you. Excuse me, lovely lady. Farewell."

"What an odd fellow," Bessian said when the surveyor had gone away.

"What shall we do now?" Diana asked.

They searched out the coachman among the thinning crowds, and he came to them as soon as they had caught his eye.

"Are we going?"

Bessian nodded.

As they turned towards their carriage, the old man put his hand on the stones that had just been set to mark the new borders, and laid a curse upon all those who might dare to move them.

Diana felt that the mountain folk, distracted for some time by the business of setting the markers, were once again turning their attention upon them. She was the first to climb into the coach, and Bessian waved for the last time to the distant figures of Ali Binak and his assistants.

Diana was a little tired, and all during the ride back to the inn she scarcely spoke.

"Shall we have some coffee before we leave?" Bessian suggested.

"If you like," Diana said.

While serving them, the innkeeper told them about famous cases of boundary disputes in which Ali Binak had been the arbitrator, the details of which had in some sort passed into the oral legendry of the mountains. You could see that he was very proud of his guest.

"When he is in these parts, he always stays at my inn."

"But where does he live?" Bessian asked, just to be saying something.

"He doesn't have any fixed residence," the innkeeper said. "He is everywhere and nowhere. He's always on the road, because there is no end to the quarrels and disputes, and people call on him to judge them."

Even after he had served them their coffee, he went on talking about Ali Binak and the centuries-old hatreds that rend mankind. He brought up the subject again when he came back to take away the cups and collect his money, and once more on accompanying them to their carriage.

Bessian was about to climb into the coach when he felt Diana press his arm.

"Look," she said softly.

A few paces away a young mountaineer, very pale, was looking at them as if dumbfounded. A black ribbon was sewn to his sleeve.

"There's a man engaged in the blood feud," Bessian said to the innkeeper. "Do you know him?"

The innkeeper's squinting eyes stared into the void a few yards to one side of the mountaineer. It was obvious that he was about to enter the inn and he had just stopped to see these persons of distinction get into their carriage.

"No," said the innkeeper. "He came by three days ago on his way to Orosh, to pay the blood-tax. "Say, young man," he called to the stranger. "What's your name?"

The young man, visibly surprised at the innkeeper's hail, turned to look at him. Diana was already inside the carriage, but Bessian paused an instant on the footboard to hear the stranger's answer. Diana's face, slightly tinged with blue by the glass, was framed in the window of the coach.

"Gjorg," the stranger replied in a rather unsteady, cracked voice, like someone who had not spoken for a very long time.

Bessian slipped down into the seat beside his wife.

"He killed a man a few days ago, and now he's coming back from Orosh."

"I heard," she said quietly, still looking out of the window.

From where he stood as if rooted to the ground, the mountaineer stared feverishly at the young woman.

"How pale he is."

"His name is Gjorg," said Bessian, settling into his seat. Diana's head was still quite close to the window. Outside, the innkeeper was lavishing advice on the coachman.

"Do you know the way? Be careful at the Graves of the *Krushks*. People always go wrong there. Instead of taking the right fork they take the left."

The carriage began to move. The stranger's eyes, that seemed very dark, perhaps because of the paleness of his face, followed the square of window where Diana's face appeared. She too, even though she knew that she should not be looking at him still, did not have the strength to turn her eyes from the wayfarer who had loomed up suddenly at the side of the road. As the coach drew away, several times she wiped away the mist that her breath left upon the glass, but it condensed again at once as if anxious to draw a curtain between them.

When the carriage had rolled a good distance, and not a soul could be seen outside, she said, leaning back wearily in her seat, "You were right."

Bessian studied his wife for a moment with a certain surprise. He was about to ask her what he had been right about, but something stopped him. To tell the truth, all during the long morning's trip he had had the feeling that on some matters she did not agree with him. And now that she was adopting his views of her own accord, it seemed superfluous, not to say imprudent, to ask her to explain herself. The main thing was that she had not found the journey a disappointment. And she had just reassured him on that point. Bessian felt enlivened. It seemed to him that he was beginning, if only vaguely, to understand more or less what it was that he had been right about.

"Did you notice how pale that mountaineer was, the one who killed a man a few days ago?" asked Bessian, staring God knows why at the ring on one of her fingers.

"Yes, he was dreadfully pale," Diana said.

"Who can tell what doubts, what hesitations he had to overcome before setting out to commit that crime. What are Hamlet's doubts, compared with this Hamlet of our mountains?"

The look she gave her husband was one of gratitude.

"You feel it's a bit much for me to call up the Danish prince in connection with a mountaineer of the High Plateau."

"Not at all," Diana said. "You put things so well, and you know how much I value that gift of yours."

The suspicion crossed his mind that it was perhaps that very gift that had won Diana for him.

"Hamlet was spurred to vengeance by his father's ghost," Bessian went on excitedly. "But can you imagine what dreadful ghost rises up before a mountaineer to spur him on to vengeance?"

Diana's eyes, grown enormously wide, looked at him fixedly.

"In houses that have a death to avenge, they hang up the victim's bloodstained shirt at a corner of the tower, and they do not take it down until the blood has been redeemed. Can you imagine how terrible that must be? Hamlet saw his father's ghost two or three times, at midnight, and for only a few moments, while the shirt that calls for vengeance in our *kullas* stays there day and night, for whole months and seasons; the bloodstains become yellow and people say, 'Look, the dead man is impatient for revenge.'"

"Perhaps that's why he was so pale."

"Who?"

"The mountaineer we saw just now."

"Oh, yes. Of course."

For a moment Bessian thought that Diana had uttered the word "pale" as if she had said "beautiful," but he dismissed the idea at once.

"And what will he do now?"

"Who?"

"Well, that mountaineer."

"Ah, what will he do?" Bessian shrugged his shoulders. "If he killed his man four or five days ago, as the innkeeper

111

said, and if he has been granted the long *bessa*, that is to say thirty days, then he still has twenty-five days of normal life before him." Bessian smiled sourly, but his face was still expressionless. "It's like a last authorization to go on leave in this world. The well-known saying that the living are only the dead on leave has a very real significance in our mountain country."

"Yes," she said, "he looked just like a man on leave from the other world, with the insignia of death on his sleeve." Diana gave a deep sigh. "You told me so—just like Hamlet."

Bessian looked through the window with a fixed smile; only the upper part of his face smiled.

"And it has to be said, too, that once Hamlet was sure of what it was he had to do, he carried out his murder in hot blood. As for him—" Bessian waved his hand at the stretch of road they were leaving behind them—"he is moved by a machine that is foreign to him, and occasionally even to the times he lives in."

Diana listened to him attentively, even though some of the import of his meaning escaped her.

"A man must have the will of a Titan to turn towards death on orders that come from a place so far away," Bessian said. "For, in point of fact, at times the orders come from a really distant place, the place of generations long gone."

Diana took a deep breath again.

"Gjorg," she said softly. "That is his name, isn't it?"

"Whose?"

"That mountaineer, of course . . . at the inn."

"Oh, yes, Gjorg. That's his name all right. He really impressed you, didn't he?"

She nodded her head.

Several times it looked as if it was going to rain, but the raindrops were lost in space before they could reach the earth. Only a few splashed on the carriage window and these quivered on the pane like tears. Diana had been watching them for some moments, and the glass itself seemed troubled.

She did not feel tired at all now. On the contrary, as if she had been unburdened within her, she felt that she had somehow grown transparent, but it was a cold sensation, not at all pleasant.

"This has been a long winter," Bessian said. "It simply refuses to yield its place to spring."

Diana was still looking at the landscape. There was something about the scene that disturbed one's attention, that emptied one's mind—by diluting one's thoughts, as it seemed. Diana thought about the examples of Ali Binak's subtle interpretations of the *Kanun* that she had heard the innkeeper recount. Actually, she remembered only certain facets or fragments of those reports, moving slowly along on the current of her thoughts. For example, two large doors of two houses were ordered lifted from their hinges and exchanged one for the other. One of those doors had been pierced by a bullet on a summer evening. The master of the house, wronged in that way, had to avenge himself for the affront, but how was he to go about it? A door holed by a bullet is not a cause for blood vengeance under the Code, and yet the offense must nonetheless be atoned for. To decide the matter, they appealed to Ali Binak, who declared that the door of the offender must be taken from its hinges and replaced by the one with the bullet hole, which that man was to keep forever.

Diana imagined Ali Binak going from village to village and from banner to banner, escorted by his two assistants.

It was hard to imagine a more curious group. And, on another night, a man who had a friend visit him unexpectedly, sent his wife to the neighbors to borrow some victuals. Hours passed, and the woman did not return, but the husband controlled himself and hid his disquiet until the morning. Well, she did not come back on that day or the next. Something without precedent had happened on the High Plateau: the three brothers who lived in the neighboring house had kept her by force, each of them spending one night with her.

Diana imagined herself in the wife's place, and she shuddered. She shook her head as if to rid herself of the horrible thought, but she could not free herself of it.

On the morning following the third night, the woman returned at last, and she told her husband everything. But what could the injured man do? It was a most extraordinary incident, and the affront could only be washed away in blood. The clan to which the three depraved brothers belonged was large and powerful, and if a feud were to start, the family of the wronged man would be doomed to annihilation. Besides, it turned out that the husband's strong point was not courage. So, given this unusual case, he asked for something that a mountaineer rarely seeks, having recourse to judgment by a council of elders. The judgment was hard to arrive at. It was awkward to pronounce on a matter that had no precedent in the memory of the people of the *Rrafsh*, and it was equally difficult to fix a punishment for the three brothers. So they called for Ali Binak, and he ended by proposing two courses to the guilty men, who were to choose between the two. Either the three brothers would send their wives in turn to spend a night with the wronged husband, or they must choose one among them who would pay for the crime with his

114

blood, and whose death could not be avenged thereafter. The brothers held a counsel and chose the second course: one of them would pay with his life for what they had done: the lot fell on the second brother.

Diana imagined the death of the second brother in slow motion as if in a film. He had asked the council of elders to grant him the thirty-day truce. Then, on the thirtieth day, the wronged man lay in wait for him and killed him with no trouble at all.

"And then?" Bessian had asked. "Then, nothing," the innkeeper said. "He lived on this earth, and then he disappeared—all that for nothing, for a whim."

Diana, on the edge of sleep, thought about the time that was left to the mountaineer named Gjorg, whose fate was already settled, and she sighed.

"Look, there's a tower of refuge," Bessian said, tapping the window pane with his finger.

Diana looked where her husband was pointing.

"That one over there, standing by itself, can you see it? The one with the narrow loopholes."

"How grim it looks," Diana said.

She had often heard talk about those famous towers, where the killers might take refuge at the end of the truce so as not to put their families in danger. But this was the first time that she had seen one.

"The tower loopholes look out on all the roads in the village, so that nobody can come near without being seen by the men immured within," Bessian told her. "And there is always one loophole that faces the church door, because of the possibility of an offer to make peace, but those cases are very few."

"And how long do people stay shut up inside?" Diana asked.

"Oh, for years, until new occurrences change the relations between the blood that has been shed and the blood that has been avenged."

"The blood that has been shed, the blood that has been avenged," Diana repeated. "You speak of those things as if they were bank transactions."

Bessian smiled.

"At bottom, in one sense, those things are not very different. The *Kanun* is cold calculation."

"That's really dreadful," Diana said, and Bessian could not tell if she had said that about the tower of refuge or about his last remark. In fact, she had pressed her face against the glass in order to see the dark tower again.

That's where that mountaineer with the pale face might take refuge, she thought. But he might be killed before he could shut himself up inside that stony mass.

Gjorg. She said the name to herself and she felt that an emptiness was spreading inside her chest. Something was coming apart painfully there, but there was a certain sweetness in it.

Diana sensed that she was losing the defenses that protect a young woman from the very idea of having strong feelings about another man during the time of her engagement or when she is very much in love. This was the first time since she had known Bessian that she allowed herself to think quite freely about someone else. She thought of *him*, the man who was still on leave in this world, as Bessian had put it, a very brief leave, scarcely three weeks and each passing day shortened it further, as he wandered in the mountains with that black ribbon on his sleeve, the sign of his blood debt that he seemed to be paying even beforehand—so pale he was—chosen by death, like a tree to be felled in the forest. And that was what his eyes had said, fixed on hers: I am here only a short time, foreign woman.

Never had a man's stare troubled Diana so much. Perhaps, she thought, it was the nearness of death, or the sympathy awakened in her by the beauty of the young mountaineer. And now she could scarcely tell whether the few drops of water on the glass were not tears in her eyes.

"What a long day," she said aloud, and was surprised at her own words.

"Do you feel tired?" Bessian asked.

"A little."

"We should be there in an hour, or an hour and a quarter at most."

He put his arm around her shoulders and drew her gently to him. She let him do that, not resisting, but she did not make herself lighter so as to let him pull her closer. He noticed, but stirred by the odor of her neck, he leaned his head towards her ear and whispered, "How are we going to sleep tonight?"

She shrugged her shoulders, as if to say, "How would I know?"

"At least the tower of Orosh is the *kulla* of a prince, and I think they will put us in the same room," he went on softly, almost conspiratorially

He looked sidelong at her face, and his expression was like the insinuating caress of his voice. But she kept her eyes before her and did not answer. Unsure whether to be offended or not, he relaxed his arm somewhat, and he would surely have taken it away completely if at the last moment, perhaps because she had guessed his intention or perhaps by accident, she had not asked him a question.

"What?"

"I asked you if the prince of Orosh is a blood relation of the royal family."

"No, not at all," he replied.

"Then how is it that he is called a prince?"

Bessian frowned a little.

"It's rather complicated," he said. "To tell the truth, he's not a prince, despite the fact that they call him one in certain circles and the people of the High Plateau call him "*Prenk*," which means prince exactly. But mostly they call him *Kapidan*, even though. . . ."

Bessian remembered he had not smoked a cigarette for quite a while. Like all those who smoke only now and then, it took some time for him to take the cigarette from the pack and the match from the little box. Diana felt that he did this whenever he wanted to put off a difficult explanation. And indeed the explanation he began to give her about the *Kulla* of Orosh (an explanation that he had left unfinished in Tirana, when from the prince's chancellory, in stilted language—really rather strange—an invitation to the *Kulla* of Orosh had reached him, saying that he would be welcome at any season of the year and at any hour of the day or the night) was no clearer than the one he had cut off then in Tirana, drinking a cup of tea, seated on the sofa in his studio. But perhaps that came from the fact that there was something unclear in everything that had to do with the *kulla* where they would soon be guests.

"He's not exactly a prince," Bessian said, "and yet, in a way, he's more than a prince, not only because of his lineage, much older than that of the royal family, but chiefly because of the way he rules over all the High Plateau."

He went on explaining that the prince's power was of a

very special kind, founded on the *Kanun* and unlike any other regime in the world. Time out of mind, neither police nor government had had any authority over the High Plateau. The castle itself had neither a police force nor governmental powers, but the High Plateau was nonetheless wholly under its control. That had been true in the time of the Turks, and even earlier, and that state of affairs had gone on under the Serbian occupation and the Austrian occupation, and then under the first republic, and the second, and now under the monarchy. Some years ago a group of deputies tried to put the High Plateau under the authority of the national government, but the attempt failed. The partisans of Orosh had said that we should act so that the *Kanun* would extend its sway over the entire country instead of trying to uproot it in the mountains, though of course no power in the world could achieve that.

Diana asked Bessian a question about the princely origins of the master of the *Kulla*, and he had the feeling that she did that in the naive way that a woman tries to find out if the jewelry someone is about to give her is really gold.

He told her that he did not believe in the princely origins of the lords of Orosh. At the very least, that matter had not been established. Their origins were lost in the mists of time. According to Bessian, there were two possibilities: either they were descendants of a very old but not very distinguished feudal family, or else they were a family that, generation after generation, had dealt in interpreting the *Kanun*. It was well known that a dynasty of that kind, which was rather like a temple of the law, an institution halfway between oracles and repositories of legal tradition, could in time amass great power, until their origins were quite forgotten and they exercised absolute dominion.

119

"I said that the family interpreted the *Kanun*," Bessian went on, "because to this day, the *Kulla* of Orosh is recognized as the guardian of that very *Kanun*."

"But isn't the family itself outside the Code?" Diana asked. "I think you told me that once."

"Yes, that is the case. It is the only family that is not under the jurisdiction of the *Kanun*."

"And there are all sorts of grim legends about it, aren't there?"

"Yes, of course. Naturally, a castle as old as this is bound to have an atmosphere of mystery."

"How interesting," Diana said, gaily this time, cuddling up to him as before. "It's so exciting to be visiting there, isn't it?"

He took a deep breath, as if after some great exertion. He pulled her close again, and he looked at her with a mixture of tenderness and reproof, as if he were telling her, why do you torment me by removing yourself so suddenly and so far, when you are so close to me?

Her face was lit once again by that smile that he could see only from the side, and that was almost entirely directed straight before her, into the distance.

He put his head to the window.

"It will be night soon."

"The tower must not be far now," Diana said.

Both were trying to find it, each looking out through the window nearest them. The late-afternoon sky was set in a heavy immobility. The clouds seemed to have frozen forever, and if some sense of motion still persisted around them, its locus was not the sky but the earth. The mountains filed by slowly before their eyes, at the same speed as their rolling carriage.

Holding hands, they searched the horizon to find the tower. The mystery of it brought them closer still. Several times they cried out almost simultaneously, "There it is! There it is!" But they knew at once that they were mistaken. It was only the mountain peaks with shreds of cloud clinging to them.

All around them was empty space. One would have thought that other buildings and life itself had withdrawn so as not to disturb the solitude of the *Kulla* of Orosh.

"But where is it?" Diana said plaintively.

Their eyes sought the tower at every point on the horizon, and it would have seemed just as natural to see it appear high in the sky, among the tattered clouds, as somewhere on the earth, among the rocky peaks.

The light of the copper lamp carried by the man who was leading them up to the third storey of the *kulla* wavered mournfully on the walls.

"This way, sir," he said for the third time, holding the lamp away from him the better to light their way. The floor was made of wooden boards that seemed to creak louder at that hour of the night. "This way, sir."

In the room, another lamp, also of copper, its wick scarcely turned up, shed a feeble light on the walls and on the pattern of the carpet on a deep red ground. Against her will, Diana sighed.

"I'll bring your suitcases at once," said the man, and he went away quietly.

They stood there for a moment, looking at each other, and then they looked around the room.

"What did you think of the prince?" Bessian asked in a low voice.

"It's hard to say," Diana replied, almost in a whisper. At any other time she would have admitted that she did not know what to make of him; he was not very natural, any more than the style of his invitation, but she felt that long explanations were out of place at that late hour. "It's hard to say," she repeated. "As for the other one, the steward of the blood, I think he's repulsive."

"I do too," Bessian said.

His eyes, and then Diana's, rested stealthily on the heavy oak bed and its heavy red woolen coverlet with a deep nap. On the wall, above the bed, there was a cross of oak.

Bessian went to one of the windows. He was still standing there when the man came back, holding his copper lamp in one hand and the two suitcases in the other.

He set them down on the floor and Bessian, his back to the man and his face pressed to the window-pane, asked, "What is that, down there?"

The man walked over with a light step. Diana watched them both for a moment, leaning on the window-sill, looking down as if into a chasm.

"It's a sort of large room, sir, a sort of gallery, I don't know what to call it, where you take in the people from all parts of the *Rrafsh* when they come to pay the blood tax."

"Oh," Bessian said. Because his face was right against the pane, his voice sounded strange to Diana. "That's the famous murderers' gallery."

"*Gjaks*, sir."

"Yes, *gjaks*. . . . I know. I've heard of them."

Bessian stayed by the window. The servant of the castle withdrew a few steps, noiselessly.

"Good night, sir. Good night, madam."

"Good night," Diana said, without raising her head that was bent over the suitcase that she had just opened. She went through her things languidly, without deciding to choose this or that. The evening meal had been heavy, and she felt an unpleasant weight in her stomach. She looked at the red woolen coverlet on the broad bed, then turned again to her suitcase, hesitating about putting on her night-gown.

She was still undecided when she heard his voice.

"Come see."

She got up and went to the window. He moved to make room for her and she felt the icy coldness of the glass go right through her. Outside, the darkness seemed to hover over an abyss.

"Look down there," Bessian said faintly.

She looked into the darkness, but saw nothing; she was penetrated with the vastness of the black night and she shivered.

"There," he said, touching the glass with his hand, "down there, don't you see a light?"

"Where?"

"Down there, all the way down."

At last she saw a glimmer. Rather than a light it was a feeble reddish glow on the rim of the abyss.

"I see," she said. "But what is it?"

"It's the famous gallery where the *gjaks* wait for days and sometimes weeks on end to pay the blood-tax."

He felt her breath come faster by his shoulder.

"Why do they have to wait so long?" she asked.

"I don't know. The *kulla* doesn't make paying the tax

easy. Perhaps so that there will always be people waiting in that gallery. You're cold. Put something over your shoulders."

"That mountaineer back there, at the inn, he must have come here, too?"

"Certainly. The innkeeper told us about him. Don't you remember?"

"Yes, that's right. It seems that he came here three days ago to pay the blood tax. That's what he told us."

"Just so."

Diana could not suppress a sigh.

"So he was here. . . . "

"Without exception, every killer on the High Plateau goes through that gallery," he said.

"That's terrifying. Don't you think so?"

"It's true. To think that for more than four hundred years, since the building of the castle of Orosh, in that gallery, night and day, winter and summer, there have always been killers waiting there."

She felt his face near her forehead.

"Of course it's frightening, it couldn't be otherwise. Murderers waiting to pay. It's truly tragic. I'd even say that in a certain way there is grandeur in it."

"Grandeur?"

"Not in the usual meaning of the word. But in any case, that glimmer in the darkness, like a candle shining on death. . . . Lord, there really is something supremely sinister about it. And when you think that it's not just a matter of the death of a single man, of a candle-end shining on his grave, but infinite death. You're cold. I told you to put something over your shoulders."

They stood there awhile, not turning their eyes from

124

that light at the foot of the *kulla*, until Diana felt chilled to her marrow.

"Brr! I'm freezing," she said, and moving away from the window she said, "Bessian, don't stay there, you'll catch cold."

He turned and took two or three steps towards the centre of the room. At that moment, a clock on the wall that he had not noticed struck twice with a deep sound that made them both start.

"Goodness, how frightened I was," Diana said.

She knelt down again to her suitcase. "I'm taking out your pyjamas," she said a moment later.

He murmured a few words and began to walk up and down the room. Diana went over to a mirror that stood on a chest of drawers.

"Are you sleepy?" she asked.

"No. Are you?"

"Me neither."

He sat down on the edge of the bed and lit a cigarette.

"It would have been better not to have had that second cup of coffee."

Diana said something, but since she had a hairpin in her mouth, he could not make out the words.

Bessian stretched out now, and leaning on his elbow, looked on distractedly at his wife's familiar gestures before the mirror. That mirror, the chest, the clock, as well as the bed and most of the other furniture of the *kulla*, were related, as their lines showed, to a baroque style, but simplified in the extreme.

As she combed her hair in the mirror, Diana watched out of the corner of her eye the wreaths of smoke floating over Bessian's abstracted face. The comb moved ever more slowly through her hair. With an unhurried gesture she put it down on the chest, and watching her husband in the mirror, quietly, as if she did not want to attract his attention, she walked with light steps to the window.

Beyond the glass was anguish and night. She let their tremors pass through her while her eyes searched insistently for the tiny lost glimmer of light in the chaos of darkness. It was there down below, in the same place, as if suspended above the chasm, flickering wanly, about to be swallowed up by the night. For a long moment she could not take her eyes from the feeble red glow in that abyss of darkness. It was like the redness of primeval fire, a magma ages old whose pallid reflection came from the centre of the earth. It was like the gates of hell. And suddenly, with unbearable intensity, the guise of the man who had passed through that hell was present to her. Gjorg, she cried out within her, moving her cold lips. He wandered forbidden roads, bearing omens of death in his hands, on his sleeve, in his wings. He must be a demigod to face that darkness and primal chaos of creation. And being so strange, so unattainable, he took on enormous size, he swelled and floated like a universal howling in the night.

Now she could not believe that she had actually seen him, and that he had seen her. Comparing herself with him she felt colorless, stripped of all mystery. Hamlet of the mountains, she thought, repeating Bessian's words. My black prince.

Would she ever meet him again? And there, by the window, her forehead icy from the frozen pane, she felt she would give anything to see him again.

Then she felt her husband's breath behind her, and his hand resting upon her hip. For some moments he gently caressed that part of her body that moved him more than any other, then, not seeing what was happening in her face, he asked her in a muffled voice, "What's the matter?"

Diana did not answer, but she kept her head turned towards the black panes, as if inviting him to look out there too.

CHAPTER IV

Mark Ukacierra was going up the wooden stairway leading to the third storey of the *kulla* when he heard a voice calling to him in a low tone, "Hush! The guests are still asleep!"

He went on his way without any attempt to lighten his footfalls, and the voice above him on the stairs, came again: "I told you not to make noise. Didn't you hear me? The guests are still asleep!"

Mark raised his eyes to see who had dared address him in that way, just as one of the servants put his head over the banister to see who had shattered the quiet. But recognizing the steward of the blood, the servant, horrified, clapped his hand over his mouth.

Mark Ukacierra went on ascending, and when he reached the top of the stairway, he passed right by the terror-stricken man without saying a word to him, not even turning his head.

Ukacierra was first cousin to the prince, and since on the roster of duties in the castle he was concerned with all the business connected with bloodshed, he was called the steward of the blood. The other servants, while for the most part also cousins of the prince, albeit distant ones, feared the steward just as much as the prince. They stared in amazement at their colleague who had so narrowly escaped a storm, and recalled, not without resentment, other occasions on which the slightest misstep had cost them dear. But the steward of the blood, even though he had dined sumptuously with distinguished guests last night, was distracted this morning. His face ashen, he was obviously out of sorts. Without glancing at any of them, he pushed open the door of a large room adjoining the living room and went in.

The room was cold. Through the panes of the high, narrow windows framed in unpainted oak, came a light that seemed to him the light of an evil day. He went closer to the windows and looked out at the motionless clouds. April was almost here, but the sky had not yet taken leave of March. That idea came to him and brought a particular sense of annoyance, as if it were an injustice aimed specifically at him.

His eyes fixed on the scene beyond the window, as if he wanted to torment them with the grey light that was quite as trying, he forgot the corridors filled with cautious steps, with "Sh! Quiet!" and the guests who had arrived last night, who had aroused in him without his taking account of it a vague disquiet.

Last night's dinner had been troublesome. He had had no appetite. Something gnawed at his stomach, gave him

130

an empty feeling that, while he forced himself to eat, seemed more empty with every mouthful.

Mark Ukacierra turned his eyes away from the windows, and looked for a moment at the heavy oak shelves of the library. Most of the books were old, religious works in Latin and in old Albanian. On another shelf set apart from these were, side by side, contemporary publications dealing directly or indirectly with the *Kanun* and the *Kulla* of Orosh. Some of the books treated these matters only, and there were journals that contained extracts, articles, monographs, and poems.

If the chief function of Mark Ukacierra was to look after the business of the blood-tax, he was also in charge of the castle's archives. The various documents were kept in the lower part of the bookcase that was lined on the inside with sheet iron as a safety measure, and locked with a key: deeds, secret treaties, correspondence with foreign consuls, agreements with the successive governments of Albania, with the first republic, the second republic, and the monarchy, agreements with the governors or military commanders of the troops of occupying powers, Turks, Serbs, Austrians. There were documents in foreign languages but for the most part they were written in old Albanian. A great padlock, whose key Mark carried hanging from his neck, glittered yellow between the two doors.

Mark Ukacierra took a step towards the bookshelves, and passed his hand half-caressingly, half-angrily along the row of books and current magazines. He could read and write, but not well enough to really understand what they said about Orosh. A monk from the convent not far from the *Kulla* came once a month to arrange, according to their contents, the books and magazines that came by the post.

131

He divided them into good and bad publications: the first were those that spoke well of Orosh and the *Kanun*, the second those that spoke ill, and the proportion of good to bad always varied. Usually the good publications were more numerous, but the number of the bad ones was by no means negligible. There were times when the bad ones increased so as to nearly equal the tally of the good.

Again, Mark passed his hand along the row of books in annoyance, and two or three fell down. There were stories, plays and legends of the High Plateau that, as the monk said, were good for the soul, but there were others bitter as poison, so that one could not understand how the prince could bear to see them on his bookshelves. If it were up to Mark Ukacierra, he would have burnt those books long ago. But the prince was easy-going. Far from burning them or throwing them out of the window, there were times when he actually leafed through them. He was the master and he knew what he was doing.

Last night after dinner, as he walked before his guests through the rooms that adjoined the great hall, he had said on coming to the library, "How many times they have spat upon Orosh, but Orosh was not shaken by it and never will be." And instead of seeing to the battlements of the *Kulla*, he would leaf through the books and periodicals as if in them he might find the secret not only of the attacks upon his stronghold but of its defense. "How many governments have fallen," the prince had gone on, "And how many kingdoms have been swept from the face of the earth, and Orosh is still standing."

And that fellow, the writer, whom Mark had not cared for from the start, no more than for his beautiful wife, he had leaned down to the books and periodicals to read their titles, and he had said nothing. In the light of what Mark thought he understood in the course of the conversation at dinner, the man had written about the *Rrafsh* himself, but in such a way that you could not tell whether it was well meant or not. A kind of hybrid. But perhaps it was just for that reason that the prince had invited him to the castle with his wife—to see what he had in mind and to persuade him to adopt his own views.

The steward of the blood turned his back on the bookshelves and looked out of the window again. As far as he was concerned, he had no faith in these guests. It was not only the vague dislike he had felt as soon as he had laid eyes on them, going up the stairs with their leather suitcases, but rather because of a different feeling that was the source of that dislike, a kind of fear that these guests, the woman in particular, aroused in him. The steward of the blood smiled bitterly. Everyone who knew him would have been astonished to learn that he, Mark Ukacierra, who had seldom been afraid of anything all his life—even things that made brave men turn pale—had felt fear in the presence of a woman. Nevertheless, there it was: she had frightened him. By her expression he had understood at once that she had doubts about certain things that were being said around the table. Some of the opinions offered—quite discreetly—by his master, the prince, which had always seemed to him to have the force of law, to be beyond discussion, quietly fell apart, annihilated, as soon as they came before that young woman's eyes. Can this be possible? Two or three times he had put the question to himself, and he had pulled himself up short immediately. No, it's not possible. It's me, I'm losing my wits. But he had glanced furtively at the young woman again, and he was certain that it was really so. The words dissolved in her eyes, lost their strength. And after the words, a wing of the *kulla* collapsed, and then himself. It was the first time that this had happened, and that was the reason for his fear. All kinds of distinguished guests had occupied the prince's guest room, from papal envoys to persons close to King Zog, and even those bearded men they call philosophers or scholars, but not one of them had stirred any such feeling in him.

Perhaps that was why the prince had talked more than usual last night. Everyone knew that he was restrained in his speech; sometimes he only opened his mouth to welcome his guests, and usually it was other people who kept the conversation going. But last night, to everyone's astonishment, he had broken his custom. And in whose presence? A woman's. Not a woman—a witch. Beautiful as the fairies of the high mountains, but evil. The first mistake was to have allowed that woman to enter the men's chamber, against all custom. The *Kanun* knew what it was doing in forbidding women to enter that room. But recently, worse luck, fashion had grown so powerful that one could sense the diabolical spirit even here, in the very pillar of the *Kanun*, at Orosh.

Mark Ukacierra felt again the nauseous hollow in his stomach. A secret spite contributed to that sick sensation, and it wanted to vent itself, but finding no proper outlet, it turned inward to make him suffer. He wanted to vomit. In fact, he had noticed for some time now that an ill wind blowing from afar, from the cities and the low country that had long ago lost their virility, was trying to stain and infect the high country too. And it had started with the appearance in the *Rrafsh* of these women dressed to kill, with chestnut or auburn hair, who stirred up a lust for life—even without honor; women who traveled in carriages that rolled along swaying from side to side, carriages of corruption, accompanied by men who were men in name only. And the worst of it was that these capricious dolls were brought right into the men's chamber, and at Orosh, no less, in the cradle of the *Kanun*. No, all that wasn't just chance. Something was blighted, something was rotting away visibly around him. And he was the one who had to account for the decline of the number of killings in the blood feud. Last night, the prince had said—rancorously, looking sidelong at him—"There are some people who would like to see the *Kanun* of our forefathers softened." What had the lord of Orosh meant by that look? Was it Mark Ukacierra who was responsible for the fact that the Code, and especially the blood feud, had shown signs of weakening recently? Couldn't he smell the stench that rose from those androgynous cities? It was true that revenues from the blood tax were smaller this year, but he was not the only person responsible, any more than the fine corn crop was solely to the credit of the bailiff. If the weather had not been in our favor, then he would have seen what the harvest was like! But the year had been good and the prince had praised the bailiff. But blood was not rain falling from the sky. The reasons for its decline were obscure. Of course he had some share of responsibility for all that. But not everything was his doing. Well, if they had given him fuller powers, and if they had let him manage things his way, then, certainly, they could take him to task about the blood tax. Then he would know how to go about it. However, while his impressive title made people tremble, his powers were limited. That was why the blood-feud and everything connected with it was in jeopardy. The number of killings had fallen year after year, and the first season of the current year had been disastrous. He had sensed that, and had awaited anxiously the accounting that his assistants had drawn up for him a few days before. The results had been even worse than he had feared: the monies collected were less than seventy percent of the revenue of the corresponding period in the preceding year. And this at a time when not only the bailiff in charge of croplands but all the other managers in the Prince's service, the bailiff for cattle and pastures, the bailiff for loans, and most of all, the bailiff for mills and mines, who attended to all the trades that required tools, from looms to forges, had payed large sums into the general treasury. As for himself, the chief bailiff (for the sums realized by the others came solely from the holdings of the castle, while his were levied upon the whole of the High Plateau) who at one time used to collect sums equal to the total of all other revenues, he now brought in only half the amount of those monies.

That was why the look that the prince had given him at dinner last night was harsher than his words. That look seemed to say, you are the steward of the blood, and therefore you ought to be the chief instigator of feuds and acts of vengeance; you ought to be encouraging them, stirring them up, whipping them on when they flag or falter.

But you do just the opposite. You don't deserve your title. That was what that look meant. O Lord, Mark Ukacierra groaned as he stood by the window. Why didn't they let him alone? Didn't he have enough trouble?

He tried to put aside his troubled thoughts, bent down to the lowest shelf of the bookcase, and pulling open the heavy door, took out a thick, leather-bound ledger. This was *The Blood Book*. For some time he leafed through the stout pages filled with dense script in double column. His eyes took in nothing, merely skimming coldly over those thousands of names, whose syllables were as alike as the pebbles of an endless beach. Here were detailed descriptions of the feuds of the entire High Plateau, the debts of death that families or clans owed to one another, the payment of those deaths by the parties concerned, the cases of vengeance not yet satisfied that would keep the feuds alive ten, twenty, sometimes one hundred and twenty years later, the unending accounts of debts and payments, of whole generations annihilated, the blood-oak (the male line, or the line of inheritance), the milk-oak (the line of the womb), blood washed away by blood, so-and-so for so-and-so, one for one, one head for another, four brace killed, fourteen, eighty, and always blood that was still to be shed; blood left over that, like the ram that leads the flock, draws after it new multitudes of the dead.

The book was old, perhaps as old as the castle. It was complete, and it was opened when people came to consult it, people sent by their family or their clan who had been living in peace for a long time, but who suddenly—because of a doubt, a supposition, a rumor, or a bad dream—felt their tranquility shaken. Then the steward of the blood, Mark Ukacierra, like some dozens of his predecessors, would open the thick pages of the book, searching page by page and column by column the spread of the blood-oak, and stop at last at one place. "Yes, you have blood to settle. In such a year, such a month, you left this debt of blood unpaid." In a case of that kind, the expression of the steward of the blood was one of stern reproach for the long period of forgetfulness. His eyes seemed to say, your peace has been a falsehood, unhappy man!

But that seldom happened. Mostly, the members of a family remembered from generation to generation every failure to avenge blood with blood. They were the living memory of the clan, and forgetting such things could only occur because of quite extraordinary events with long-lasting effects, like natural catastrophes, wars, migrations, plagues, when death was devalued, losing its grandeur, its rules, its loneliness, becoming something common and familiar, ordinary, insignificant. In some such flood of death, drear and turbid, it could happen that a debt of vengeance was forgotten. But even if that happened, the book was always there, under lock and key in the *Kulla* of Orosh, and the years might pass, the family flourish and put out new shoots, and then one day the doubt would arise, the rumor, or the mad dream that would bring everything to life again.

Mark Ukacierra went on leafing through the ledger. His eyes paused at the years of harvest for the blood feud, or again at the years of famine. Although he had seen the notations and compared them many, many times before, in going through them now he shook his head uncomprehendingly. That head-shaking was at once a complaint and a threat, as if he were secretly inveighing against the times gone by. Here were the years 1611-1628, that tallied the largest number of killings in the whole seventeenth century. And here was the year 1639, with the lowest count: 722 murders in all for the High Plateau. That was the dreadful year in which there were two insurrections, when seas of blood had been shed—but that was blood of another sort, not the blood of the *Kanun*. Then, one after the other, the years 1640 to 1690, an entire half-century in which, year by year, the blood that had once flowed in a torrent flowed scarcely at all, in droplets. One would have thought that the blood-feud was coming to an end. But just when the killings seemed to stop completely, they came back in force. The year 1691: double the previous

138

year's toll of vengeance. In 1693 the number tripled. In 1694 it quadrupled. The Code had undergone a basic transformation. The duty of exacting vengeance from the perpetrator of a murder was now extended to his whole family. The last years of that century and the first of the following one were drenched in blood. That condition prevailed until the middle of the eighteenth century, at which time there was another era of drought. Then came the famine year of 1754. Then 1799. A century later, three years—1878, 1879, 1880—were years of revolutions or wars against foreigners, and the number of blood-feud killings fell. The blood spilled in the course of these wars was foreign to the *Kulla* of Orosh and to the *Kanun*, and accordingly these were the *gjakhups** years.

But the spring season of this current year could not possibly be worse. He came close to trembling when he remembered the seventeenth of March. Seventeenth of March, he said to himself. If that killing had not taken place at Brezftoht, there would have been no blood vengeance at all on that day. It would have been the first day of its kind—a blank—in a century, perhaps during two, three, five centuries, perhaps from the time of the origin of the blood feud. And now as he leafed through the ledger, it seemed to him that his hands were shaking. Look, on March 16, there were eight murders; eleven on the eighteenth; the nineteenth and the twentieth, five each; while the seventeenth had just missed being without a single death. At the very idea that such a day might come about, Mark was terror-stricken.· And to imagine that it just might have happened. That dreadful thing would indeed

---

* From the Albanian *gjak*: blood, and *hup*: to lose; that is, when the blood was lost, when one was not obliged to engage in the blood feud.

have come to pass if a certain Gjorg from Brezftoht had not arisen and bloodied that day of the Lord. He had saved the day. So that, when he had come last night to pay the blood tax, Mark Ukacierra had looked into his eyes with compassion, with gratitude, so much so that the young man was taken aback.

At last he set down the ledger on the highest shelf of the bottom compartment of the bookcase. For the tenth time, his eyes skimmed over the contemporary books and journals. When the person who was in charge of the collection put those works in order, sometimes he would read to Mark snatches of the writings of the enemies of the *Kanun*. Mark was astonished and enraged that passages of the Code and even the *Kulla* of Orosh were attacked almost openly. Hm, read me the rest, Mark grunted, interrupting the man. And his mounting rage caught up in its whirlwind not just the people who wrote such horrors, such shameless things, but all the people of the cities and the plains, and the cities and the lowlands themselves, not to say all the flatlands of all the countries of the world.

Sometimes his curiosity made him listen hours on end to what was being said there, as in the case of a discussion sponsored by one of the journals, on the question of whether the Code and its severe prescriptions had the effect of inciting the blood feud or putting obstacles in its way. Certain writers held that a number of basic articles of the *Kanun*, like the one stating that blood was never lost and could only be redeemed by blood, were open incitements to the blood feud, and in consequence barbarous. On the other hand, some wrote that those articles, apparently monstrous, were in reality most humane, since the law of retaliation in itself tended to dissuade a possible murderer by warning him; it said: Shed no blood if you do not wish to spill your own.

Mark could bear that kind of writing, but there were other sorts that drove him mad. One such article—absolutely criminal—that made the prince sleepless for many nights, and had even been accompanied by calculations that amounted to bookkeeping, had been published anonymously four months ago by one of those accursed journals. In the table presented were the figures, astonishingly accurate, of all the revenues under the heading of blood tax collected by the castle of Orosh in the course of the last four years; they were compared with other sources of income: those from corn, from cattle, from the sale of land, from loans at high interest—and senseless conclusions had been drawn from those figures. One of these was that, supposedly, the general decline that was the hallmark of our own era was reflected in the decay of such keystones of the *Kanun* as the *bessa*, the blood feud, the status of one's guest, which having been at one time elements of sublimity and grandeur in Albanian life had become denatured in the course of time, changing gradually into an inhuman machine, to the point of being reduced at last, according to the author of the article, to a capitalist enterprise carried on for the sake of profit.

The author of that article had made use of many foreign expressions that Mark could not understand, and the monk who was in charge of the library had explained them to him patiently. Such, for example, were the terms "blood industry," "blood merchandise," "blood-feud mechanism." As for the title, it was monstrous: "Blood-feudology."

Naturally, the prince, through his agents in Tirana, had

succeeded in having the journal promptly banned, but despite all his efforts, he could not learn the author's name. The ban on the periodical did not calm Mark Ukacierra. The fact that things like that could be written at all, or even conceived by the human mind, was dreadful to him.

The big clock on the wall struck seven. Again he drew near the windows, and standing there, his eyes staring in the direction of the high peaks, he felt his brain empty itself of his heavy thought. But, as usual, the emptiness was temporary. Slowly, his mind filled itself again with a cloudy grey mass. Something more than mist and less than thought. Something in between, troubling, enormous, incomplete. As soon as one part of it revealed itself, another covered it over immediately. And Mark felt that the state of mind that had invaded him might last for hours, even days.

It was not the first time that his mind had frozen in that way, faced with the riddle of the High Plateau. That part of the world was the only permissible one, normal and reasonable. The other part of the world, "down there," was a marshy hollow in the earth that gave off foul vapors and the atmosphere of degeneracy.

Motionless at the window, as so often in the past, he tried vainly to take in by thinking of it all the endless expanse of the *Rrafsh*, which began in the heart of Albania and reached just beyond the frontiers of the country. All of the High Plateau, to which in a sense he was linked by the fact that the blood taxes came to him from everywhere, was nonetheless an enigma. The bailiff in charge of croplands and vineyards, and the bailiff for mines—they had an easy task: The corn or the vine stricken with rust could be detected simply by sight, and that was true, too, of the condition of the mines, whereas the fields that had fallen to him to manage were quite invisible. Every once in a while, he thought he was just about to pierce the mystery, to lay hold of it in his imagination so as to resolve it once and for all, but slowly, as the clouds move insensibly in the sky, it escaped him. Then he returned in his thought to the fields of death, in a vain struggle to discover the secret of their fertility or their barrenness. But their drought was of a different sort, often manifesting itself in wet weather and in winter, and all the more terrible by that very fact.

Mark Ukacierra sighed. Staring at the horizon, he tried to imagine the endless spaces of the *Rrafsh*. The High Plateau had an abundance of streams, of deep gullies, snow, prairies, villages, churches, but none of that was of interest to him. For Mark Ukacierra, all of the great plateau was divided in two parts only—the part that engendered death, and the part that did not. The portion that bore death, with its fields, its objects, and its people, passed slowly before him in his mind, as it had often done: There were tens of thousands of irrigation canals, large and small, running from west to east, or from south to north, and on their banks there had sprung up countless quarrels that gave rise to feuds; hundreds of mill-races, thousands of landmarks, and these gave birth easily to disputes, and then blood-vengeance; tens of thousands of marriages, some of which were dissolved for one reason or another, but which brought one thing only—mourning; the men of the High Plateau themselves, formidable, hot-tempered, who played with death as if they were playing a game on Sunday; and so on. As for the sterile portion of the region, it was equally vast, with its cemeteries that, satiated with death, seemed to refuse any more corpses, since murder, brawling, or mere argument were prohibited within their confines. There were the *gjakhups*, those

143

persons that because of the way in which they had been killed or because of the circumstances of their death, the *Kanun* decreed unworthy of being avenged; the priests, who did not fall within the scope of the rules of blood vengeance; and all the women of the High Plateau, who did not fall within their scope either.

At times, Mark had thought of mad things that he dared not confess to anyone. Oh, if only the women as well as the men were subject to the rules of blood-letting. Then he was ashamed, even terrified—but that seldom happened, only sometimes at the end of the month or the quarter, when he felt despondent because of the figures in the ledger. Weary as he was, he would try to put those ideas from him, but his mind could find no respite and he went back to them. But this time, in going back to them, it was not to blaspheme the *Kanun* but simply to give vent to his astonishment. He thought it very strange that weddings, which were usually occasions for joy, often brought about quarrels that led to feuding, while funerals, which were necessarily sad, never led to anything of the kind. That led him to compare the ancient blood-feuds with those of recent times. On both sides of the comparison, there was both good and bad. The old feuds, just like fields that had been tilled for a long time, were dependable, but rather cold and slow to bear. Contrarily, the new feuds were violent, and sometimes they brought about as many deaths in a single year as the old ones in two decades. But since they were not deep-rooted, they might easily be brought to a stop by a reconciliation, while those of olden times were very hard to bring to a settlement. Successive generations had been accustomed to the feuds from their cradles, and so, not being able to conceive of life without them, it never entered their minds to try to free themselves from their destined end. It was not for nothing that people said, "Blood-letting that lasts twelve years is like the oak, hard to uproot." In any case, Mark Ukacierra had come to the conclusion that the two kinds of feud, the ancient one rooted in history, and the new one with its vitality, had somehow joined together, and the exhaustion of the one sort had affected the other. That was why for some time now, for example, it was hard to understand which of the two had begun to weaken first. O Lord, he said aloud, if things go on like this it will be my undoing.

The first stroke of the clock startled him. He counted. . . . six, seven, eight. Behind doors, in the hallways, only the light rustling of brooms could be heard. The guests were still asleep.

The daylight, even though it was brighter now, still looked cold and hostile as the far spaces from which it came. Lord, he sighed, this time so deeply that he felt as if his ribs were creaking like the timbers of a hut that someone was trying to tear down. His eyes were fixed on the gray sky that spread, lonely, above the mountains; it was hard to tell whether he was making them turn dark or if the darkness within him came from them.

His expression was at once questioning, threatening, and prayerful. What's wrong with you, he seemed to be saying to the scene before his eyes, why have you changed so.

He had always thought that he knew his *Rrafsh*, of which it was said that it was one of the largest and most sombre of the high plateaus of Europe, and that besides spreading over thousands of square miles in Albania it went beyond her frontiers, through the Albanian districts of Kosovo, those that the Slavs called "Old Serbia," but were really part of the High Plateau. That is what he used to think, but lately he found more and more that there was something about it that estranged him from it. His mind wandered painfully towards its slopes, skirted its chasms, as if he wanted to discover from whence came that incomprehensible something— worse than incomprehensible, ironic, in broad daylight. Especially when the wind began to howl and those mountains huddled together, he found them completely foreign.

He knew that the machinery of death was there, set up from time immemorial, an ancient mill that worked day and night, and whose secrets he, the steward of the blood, knew better than anyone. And yet, that did not help him drive away that feeling of estrangement. Then, as if to convince himself that it was not so, feverishly he traversed in his imagination that cold expanse unfolding in his head in a peculiar form, something between a topographical map and a cloth spread for the funeral feast.

Right now he was calling up that dismal map, looking through the library windows. In strict order, his mind arrayed all of the fertile fields of the High Plateau. They were divided into two large groups: cultivated fields, and fields lying fallow because of the blood feud. That disposition of things corresponded to a simple rule: The people who had blood to redeem tilled their fields because it was their turn to kill, and accordingly, no one threatened them, they could go out to their fields when they pleased. On the other hand, those who owed blood left the fields untilled, and immured themselves in the tower of refuge for protection. But that situation changed abruptly as soon as those who had blood to redeem had committed their murder. Then, from a family with blood to redeem, they changed into a family that owed blood, and therefore, they became *gjaks* and betook themselves to the towers of refuge, letting their fields lie fallow. Conversely, of course, their enemies ceased to be *gjaks*, they left the towers in which they had been cloistered, and since it was now their turn to kill, they were not afraid and they set about cultivating their fields just as they chose. And that state of affairs lasted until the next murder was done. Then everything was reversed again.

Whenever he travelled in the mountains on business concerning the *Kulla*, Mark Ukacierra was always attentive to the connection between the cultivated fields and the fields that lay fallow. The former were generally more extensive. They made up nearly three-quarters of all the grain fields. In some years, however, the ratio changed and was more favorable to the fields lying fallow. Those fields reached a third or two-fifths of the total number, even rising on occasion so as to equal the area of the cultivated fields. People remembered two years in which the area of the fallow fields was greater than that of the cultivated fields. Yes, but that was a long time ago. Little by little, with the decline of the blood feud, the fallow fields shrank in number. Those fields were the special joy of Mark Ukacierra. They bore witness to the power of the *Kanun*. Whole clans allowed their fields to go uncultivated and themselves to suffer hunger so that the blood might be redeemed, and contrarily there were families who did just the opposite, putting off the redemption of blood from season to season and from year to year, to gather enough corn so as to be able to cloister themselves for a long time. You are free to choose between keeping your dignity as a man and losing it, the *Kanun* said. Each man chose between corn and vengeance. Some, to their shame, chose corn, others, on the contrary, vengeance.

Mark Ukacierra had had many opportunities to see, side

by side, the fields of families engaged in the blood feud with each other.

And the picture was always the same: one field being worked here, another lying fallow there. The clods in the tilled fields struck Mark Ukacjerra as something shameful. And the vapor that rose from them, and its smell, and its quasi-feminine softness made him sick. But the neighboring fallow fields with their irregularities that sometimes looked like wrinkles and sometimes like clenched jaws, nearly moved him to tears. And everywhere in the high country, the picture was the same—cultivated fields and fields untilled, on one side of the road or the other, close but estranged, looking at each other with hatred. And what was even more peculiar was that one or two seasons later their positions would be interchanged; the fallow fields suddenly grew fertile, and the tilled fields lay fallow.

Perhaps for the tenth time that morning, Mark Ukacierra sighed. His thoughts were still far away. From the fields he turned to the roads, which he had travelled afoot or on horseback in the service of the *Kulla*. The Grand Highway of the Accursed Peaks, The Road of Shadow, the Road of the Black Drin River, the Road of the White Drin River, the Bad Road, the Great Highway of the Banners, the Road of the Cross—all these were travelled day and night by the people of the High Plateau. Special stretches of road were safeguarded by the perpetual *bessa*; that is, whoever committed a murder on those sections of roadway would incur the vengeance of a whole community. In that way, on the Grand Highway of the Banners, the section from Peter's Bridge to the Big Sycamores was under the *bessa* of the Nikaj and the district of Shala. Whoever was wronged there would be avenged by the district of the Nikaj or the district of Shala. Likewise, on the Road of Shadow, the stretch from the Fields of Reka to the Deaf Man's Mill was covered by the *bessa*. The Road of the Curraj as far as Cold Stream also benefited from the *bessa*. The manor houses of the Nikaj and of Shala were also protected by the *bessa* as well as the Old Inn on the Road of the Cross, except for its stable. The same was true of the Young Widow's Inn, with four hundred paces of roadway from its north door, from the eight ravines of the Fairies' Stream within a radius of forty paces; and the manor houses of Rreze; and the Storks' Pasture.

He tried to recall one by one the other places protected by a special *bessa*, as well as those places that were under the *bessa* of everyone—that is to say, where it was forbidden to take vengeance, as was the case of all the mills without exception, and their surroundings within a radius of forty paces, and again of the waterfalls and their surroundings within a radius of four hundred paces, because the noise of the mills or the sound of falling water would not allow a person to hear the warning cry of the avenger. The *Kanun* had thought of everything. Often, Mark Ukacierra had wondered if such places protected by the *bessa* set limits to feuding or on the contrary helped to increase the number of such encounters. Sometimes it seemed to him that because of the protection afforded every passerby, such places put death aside, but sometimes he thought that on the contrary the very road or inn that was under the *bessa*, because of its promise to avenge the blood of whomever might be killed there, led to new feuds. In his mind, all this was vague and ambiguous, like many other things in the *Kanun*.

In the past, he had asked himself the same question about the many ballads on the theme of the blood-feud which were sung all over the High Plateau. There were many bards in the villages of the various districts. There was no road on which one did not meet them, and no inn in which one could not hear them. It was hard to say if the ballads increased or diminished the numbers of the dead. They did both. One could say the same about the tales that went from mouth to mouth concerning things that had occurred in olden times or more recently, recounted during the winter nights by the fireside which would spread abroad thereafter, just as the travellers did, and come back transformed on some other night, just as a former guest might come back changed by the passing of time. Sometimes he found parts of those stories published in those sickening periodicals, strung out along their columns as if in coffins. For Mark Ukacierra, what was printed in books was only the corpse of what was recounted orally, or accompanied by the sound of the *lahoute*.*

In any case, like it or not, these things were connected with his work. Two weeks ago, the prince, preparing to give him a dressing down about the unfavorable condition of affairs, had told him so directly. As it happened, his words were a bit obscure, but the gist of it was more or less like this: If you, the steward of the blood, are tired of your work, don't forget that there are plenty of people who would be happy to have the post—and not just anybody, but university men.

It was the first time that the prince had mentioned the University in a somewhat threatening tone. On some earlier occasions, he had suggested that Mark study, with the help of the priest, every matter concerned with the blood-feud, but this time his tone had been cutting. And now that it had come to mind again, Mark Ukacierra

---

* A musical instrument having a long neck and a single string.

could feel a kind of pressure in his temples. Go ahead, engage one of those educated men who stink of perfume and give him my job, he growled. Take on a steward of the blood who is educated, and when your little effeminate steward goes mad in his third week, then you'll remember Mark Ukacierra.

For a while he let his thoughts go freely from one possible outcome to another, but they all ended in the same way—the prince would be sorry, and he himself would be triumphant. But one way or the other, I must take a tour through the whole of the High Plateau, he said to himself when he felt the flood of that brief euphoria ebb away. It would be a good idea to prepare a report for the prince's eye, like the one he had made four years ago, giving precise data about the current situation and forecasts of future conditions. Perhaps the prince's personal business was not going well either, and Mark Ukacierra was serving as his scapegoat. But that did not matter. The prince was his master, and it was not for the steward to sit in judgment of him. His anger had left him completely. His mind, whose sudden access of resentment had put him momentarily under stress, was now freed of its troubles, and it was wandering in the distance once more, among the mountains. Yes, he really must go on that journey. The more so because just now he was not feeling well. Perhaps a change of air would lighten somewhat his recent troubles. And perhaps he might be able to sleep again. Besides, it would be useful to disappear for a time from the prince's sight.

Planning that trip, without any special enthusiasm, began, little by little, stubbornly, to absorb him. And again, just as it had been a little while back, his thoughts began to untangle the roads that he would perhaps be taking, except that this time, connecting them in his mind with his boots or his horse's shoes, he thought of them in a different way; he imagined in another fashion the inns and the houses where he might sleep, the horses whinnying at night, the bedbug bites.

It would be a working trip, in the course of which he would perhaps have to review everything that was connected, in his mind, with a rough sketch of a death-mill, with its millstones, its special tools, its countless wheels and gears. He would have to examine the entire mechanism minutely in order to find what it was that was blocking its action, what was rusted and what was broken.

Oh! he exclaimed, at the sudden pain of a stomach cramp, and he was tempted to say, you would do better to look at what is broken inside you, but he did not follow his thought to the end. Perhaps a change of air would rid him as well of the nauseous hollow in his stomach that was plaguing him. Yes, he ought to set out at once, leave this place, observe everything closely, discuss things at length—especially with the interpreters of the *Kanun*, ask their opinion—visit the towers of refuge, meet with the priests, ask them if there were any persons who grumbled about the Code and if so take down their names in order to ask the prince to expel them, etc. Mark Ukacierra's spirits rose. Yes, certainly, he could draw up a detailed report on all those matters. Mark began to walk to and fro in the library. Sometimes he stopped before one of the windows; then, as a new idea occurred to him, he took up his pacing again. Already he could see the interpreters of the Code, by whose opinions the prince always set great store. There were some two hundred of them throughout the High Plateau, but only a dozen were famous. He must meet with at least half of those whose reputations were preeminent. They were the pillars of the *Kanun*, the intelligence of the High Plateau; they would certainly give their opinion of the state of affairs, and perhaps some advice about the means of improving it. But he must not rest content with that alone. His instinct told him that it would be useful to descend to the terrain that was the foundation of death, the murderer himself. He must enter the towers of refuge, speak one by one with each of the cloistered men, those who were the bread and salt of the *Kanun*. That last idea gave him special pleasure. Whatever words of wisdom might be uttered by the famous interpreters, the last word concerning death—so says the *Kanun*—belongs to the avengers of blood.

He rubbed his forehead, trying to recall the findings he had accurately reported four years ago. There were seventy-four towers of refuge in all the High Plateau, and about a thousand men cloistered in them. He tried to call up those towers in imagination, scattered, dark, forbidding, with their black loopholes and their heavy doors. Their image was bound up with that of the irrigation ditches, because of which some of those men were immured in the towers, and that was true also of those roads and inns protected by the *bessa*, and the interpreters of the *Kanun*, the story-tellers and the bards. Those were the screw mechanisms, the transmission belts, the gearwheels of the ancient machine that had worked without a stop for hundreds of years. For hundreds of years, he said again. Every day, every night. Without ever stopping. Summer and winter. But then came that day, the seventeenth of March, to disturb the order of things. Thinking of that day, Mark Ukacierra sighed once more. He felt that if that day had really passed as it very nearly had, all of that mill of death, its wheels, its heavy millstones, its many springs and gears, would make an ominous grating sound, would shake from top to bottom, and break and smash into a thousand pieces.

O Lord, may that day never come, he said, and again he felt that sensation in the hollow of his stomach. Then, mixed with the nausea, there came to mind once more some few passages of last night's dinner, the prince's discontent. And the animation he had felt for a few moments fell away completely, giving way to a strange anguish of mind. Let everything go to hell, he said. His uneasiness was of a very special kind, like a damp, gray mass that invaded him everywhere, softly, without any sharp edges nor painful pinchings. Oh, he would infinitely prefer an obvious pain, but what could he do against that pulp that he could not get rid of? People went on crushing him as if his own distress, which he never mentioned to a soul, were not enough. For three weeks now, he had been feeling it more and more frequently. All at once he asked himself the question that he had been putting off from day to day, night after night: Could he have been stricken with blood-sickness?

It had happened to him seven years ago. He had consulted doctors and taken all sorts of medication, but nothing helped, until the day when an old man from Gjakova said to him, "It's useless, my son, to take medicines and to consult doctors. Neither the doctors nor the medicines can do anything about your sickness. You are blood-sick." Mark was astonished. "Blood? I haven't killed anyone, father." And the old man answered, "It doesn't matter that you haven't killed anyone. Your work is of such a nature that you have been stricken with blood-sickness." And he spoke to him about other stewards of the blood who had been stricken with that sickness, and what was

154

worse, never recovered from it. Well, Mark had managed to cure himself in the mountains that rise beyond Orosh. The air, in those heights, was good for that kind of sickness.

For seven years, Mark had been untroubled by it, and it was only recently that his illness had come back. What was I thinking of when I took up this kind of work? The blood of one man, when it took you, was hard to overcome, but what could you do about blood that comes from who knows where, and stops flowing who knows where? It was not the blood of a single man, but torrents of the blood of generations of human beings that streamed all over the High Plateau, the blood of young men and old men, for years and for centuries.

But perhaps it isn't that sickness that I have, he sighed from deep within him in a last glimmer of hope. Maybe it's just a passing thing—if not, I'll go crazy. He listened, because he thought he heard steps beyond the door. In fact, the squeaking of a door reached him from the hallway, and then the sound of footsteps and of voices.

The guests must be awake now, he thought.

CHAPTER V

Gjorg was back in Brezftoht on the twenty-fifth of March. He had walked all day without stopping. In contrast to his journey to Orosh, he did the return trip in a semi-somnolent state, so that the road seemed shorter. He was surprised to see the outskirts of his village so soon. Without knowing why, he slowed his pace. His heart beat more slowly too, and his eyes seemed to study the surrounding hills. The snow has melted, he thought. But the wild pomegranate shrubs were still there. Despite everything, he breathed as if he felt relieved. For whatever reason, he had thought the patches of snow would be pitiless to him.

And there was the place. A small *mouranë* had been heaped up during his absence. Gjorg stopped in front of it. For an instant he felt that he was about to leap towards it, pull away the stones, and spread them about on every side so as to leave no trace of it. At the same time that his brain was imagining that act, his hand was groping feverishly for a pebble on the roadway. At last he found one, and his hand, moving awkwardly as if it were dislocated, tossed the pebble onto the cairn. The stone struck it with a dull sound, rolled over two or three times on its axis and settled among the others. Gjorg kept eyeing it as if he were afraid that it would shift again, but now it seemed that it was in its natural place, as if it had been thrown there long ago. And still, Gjorg did not stir.

He stared at the cairn. Here's what's left of . . . of . . . (he meant to say, the other man's life), but within him he thought, here's what will be left of my own life.

All that torment, sleepless nights, the silent struggle with his father, his own hesitations, his brooding, his suffering, had brought about nothing more than these meaningless bare stones. He tried to leave them behind him, but he could not stir. The world about him began to dissolve swiftly, everything disappeared; he, Gjorg, and the cairn, were the only things left on the surface of the earth. Why? What had it all amounted to? The question was bare as the stones. It hurt him everywhere. Lord, how it hurt! At last he found the strength to move, to tear himself away, to flee as far as possible, even if the farthest place was hell, anywhere, rather than stay where he was.

Gjorg's people greeted him with quiet warmth. His father asked him briefly about his journey, his mother watched him furtively with her eyes turned aside. He said that he was very tired after the long walk and his long sleeplessness, and he went to bed. For a long moment, the steps and the whispering in the *kulla* clawed at his sleep, and then he went under. The next morning, he woke late. Where am I? he asked two or three times, and he fell asleep again. When at last he got up, his head was heavy and felt as if it were stuffed with sponge. He was not up to doing anything. Not even thinking.

The day passed, and the next day and the next. He went through the house several times, noticing listlessly a section of the wall that had been in need of repair for a long time, or a corner of the roof that had fallen in during the winter. He had no heart for work. The worst of it was that any repair seemed useless to him.

It was during the last days of March. April would soon be coming in. With the first half white and the other half black. Aprildeath. If he did not die, he would be languishing in the tower of refuge. His eyes would weaken in the darkness, so that one way or the other, even if he was still alive, he would never see the world again.

After those somnolent days, his thoughts began to stir. And the first thing that his mind began to seek was a way of keeping himself from death and blindness. There was only one way, and he thought about it at great length: to be an itinerant woodcutter. That was the customary trade for mountaineers who left the High Plateau. With an axe on their shoulder (they slipped the handle under their tunic, while the axe-head, with its sharp edge shiny black, appearing behind their neck, looked like a fish's fin), they went from town to town giving an air of purpose to their wandering with the long-drawn mournful cry, "Any wood to cut?" No, it would be better to stay in the realm of Aprildeath (now he was sure that the word, which was in his mind only, was understood, and of course used, by everyone), than to go down there, in the rain-soaked cities, a hapless woodcutter run aground on barred air-holes always covered with a kind of black dust (once in the city of Shkoder he had seen a mountaineer splitting fire-wood by a barred ventilator of that sort). No, never—

better Aprildeath.

One morning, on the next-to-the-last day of March, as he went down the stone stairway of the *Kulla*, he found himself face to face with his father. He wanted to avoid having a silence settle upon them, but it did. And from behind that silence, as if from behind a wall, these words came:

"Well, Gjorg, what did you want to tell me?"

He answered, "Father, I'd like to go and wander around during the days I have left."

His father looked into his eyes for a long moment, saying nothing. Really, Gjorg thought sleepily, it's not important. At bottom, it wasn't worth wrangling again with his father over that. They had argued enough, without speaking, up to this very day. Two weeks earlier, two weeks later, that made no real difference. He could do without seeing the mountains. To tell the truth, the preference that he had expressed was foolish. He started to say, no, it's useless, father, but his father had already gone upstairs.

He came down again in a few moments, a purse in his hand. Compared to the purse that had held the money for the blood-tax, it was quite small. His father handed it to him.

"Go on, Gjorg. And have a good trip."

Gjorg took the purse.

"Thanks, father."

His father did not shift his eyes from him. "But don't forget," he said in a low voice, "your truce is over on the seventeenth of April." And he said again, "Don't forget, my son."

Gjorg wandered for several days in the district. All sorts

of roads. Inns strung along the highways. The faces of strangers. Although he had been shut up for so long in his village, he had always thought of the rest of the *Rrafsh* as being somehow frozen, especially in winter, but it was not like that at all. The High Plateau was a busy place. A continual stream of people flowed from its extremities to its center or the other way round. Some traveled in one direction, others in the opposite direction; some went uphill, some came down; and most went uphill and came downhill in the course of the same trip, and they did it so many times that at the end of their road they could not tell whether they were higher or lower than the place from which they had come.

Sometimes Gjorg thought of how the days were going by. The movement of time seemed very strange to him. Up to a certain hour, the day seemed endless to him, then, suddenly, like a drop of water that after having trembled a moment on the flower of a peach tree, falls suddenly, the day would shatter and die. April had come in, but spring was hardly in possession of things. At times, the sight of a bluish band stretching above the Alps depressed him unbearably. Well, here's April, the travellers striking up acquaintance in the inns said everywhere. It's time the spring was here. In fact, it's very late this year. Then he thought of his father's warning about the end of the truce, or rather, not all of his warning, nor even a part of it, but just the words, "my son" at the end, and at the same time, the part of the month from the first to the seventeenth of April, and the idea that everyone had a whole April, while his was amputated, chopped off. Then he tried not to think of that, and he listened to the stories of the travellers, who, to his surprise, even if they had no bread or salt in their wallets, were never short of stories.

161

In the inns you heard a swarm of facts and anecdotes about all sorts of people and times. He always stayed somewhat in the background and, pleased not to be disturbed by anyone, just lent an ear to what was being said. Sometimes his mind wandered, tried to seize bits of stories so as to fit them to his own life, or on the contrary, to join bits of his own life to the stories of other people, but that piecing together was not always easy to bring about.

And things might have gone on in this way to the end of his journey, if not for chance. One day, at an inn called The New Inn (most of the inns were named either The Old Inn or The New Inn), he heard mention of a carriage. A carriage that was lined inside with black velvet. A carriage from the city with very ornate decorations. Could it be she, he wondered, and he strained to hear. Yes, it was certainly she. Now they were talking about a beautiful woman from the city with fine eyes and auburn hair.

Gjorg started. He looked about him, scarcely knowing why. It was a room in an inn, dirty, with a sharp odor of smoke and wet wool, and as if that was not enough, the mouth that talked about that woman gave off at the same time a bad smell of tobacco and onions. Gjorg turned his eyes in every direction, as if to say, wait a minute, is this a fit place to bring up her name? But they went on talking and laughing. Gjorg was like a man in a trap, in a state between listening and not-listening, and with a ringing in his ears. And suddenly it came to him in complete clarity why it was he had undertaken this journey. He had tried to hide it from himself. He had dismissed it from his mind obstinately, had suppressed it, but the reason why was right there, in the center of his being: if he had set out on the road, it wasn't to look at the mountains, but to see that woman again. Without being aware of it, he had been

162

looking for that carriage with the strange outlines, that rolled and rolled forever across the High Plateau, while he, from far away, murmured to it, "Why do you wander through these parts, butterfly-carriage?" In reality, with its gloomy appearance, bronze door-handles, and complicated lines, the carriage reminded him of a coffin that he had seen at one time, when he had been on his only journey to Shkoder, in the Cathedral, between a funeral cortege and solemn organ music. And inside that carriage, butterfly-coffin, were the eyes of the woman with the auburn hair, that he had breathed in with a sweetness and an emotion that he had never felt in the presence of any other being in the world. He had looked into women's eyes in his life, and many of those eyes, ardent, bashful, stirring, delicate, artful, or proud, had looked into his, but never eyes like those. They were at once distant and close, understandable and enigmatic, unmoved and sympathetic. That glance, while it aroused desire, had some quality that took hold of you, carried you far away, beyond life, beyond the grave, to where you could look upon yourself with serenity.

In the night (that fragments of sleep tried to fill in disorder, as a few stars try to people a dark autumn sky), that look was the only thing that his sleep did not blot out. It remained there, at his very center, a lost jewel in whose making all the light of the world had been consumed.

Yes, it was to meet those eyes again that he had set out across the High Plateau. And these men talked about that woman as an everyday matter, in that dirty inn, in the acrid smoke, with their mouths filled with bad teeth. Suddenly, he jumped to his feet, unslung the rifle from his shoulder, and fired at them once, twice, three times, four times. He killed them all, then killed those who came to their rescue, at the same time as the innkeeper and the police who just happened to be there, then ran out and fired again at his pursuers, at still others, at whole villages that were hunting him, at the Banners, at the Provinces. All that he imagined, while in fact he did nothing more than get up and leave. The cold wind was grateful on his forehead. He stood still for a moment, his eyes half-closed, and without being able to account for it, he remembered a phrase that he had heard once, several years ago, on a damp September day, while standing in a long line of people that had formed in front of a warehouse for corn belonging to the sub-prefecture: "It seems that the young women in the city kiss you on the lips."

Since his attention, in the course of his wanderings, was constantly distracted by one thing or the other, Gjorg felt more and more that his journey was fragmentary, interrupted by periods of utter vacancy and great discontinuities. Often he was surprised to find himself on a road or at an inn when he had thought he was still on the road or at the inn which in fact he had left behind hours ago. In that way, hour by hour and day by day, his mind was breaking away from reality, and his ramblings came to seem a journey in a dream.

Now he no longer hid from himself that he was hoping to find that carriage. He did not even conceal it from others. He had inquired several times, "You didn't happen to see a carriage with a curious body with odd lines. . . . it's hard to explain." "How's that again?" they said. "Describe it. What sort of carriage?" "Well, it's very different, with black velvet inside, and bronze ornaments—like a coffin." And they said, "Are you serious? You wouldn't be a bit off your nut, would you, old fellow?"

Once someone told him that he had seen a carriage that looked something like the one Gjorg had described, but he said it was the carriage of the bishop of the next district, who was travelling, oddly enough, in very bad weather.

They can put up in these filthy inns if they like, and even have bad teeth, as long as they mention her, he said to himself.

Several times he thought he had picked up their traces, but he lost them again. The approach of death made him wish even more for that meeting. And the long way he had come also sharpened his hunger to see her.

One day he saw a man in the distance who appeared to be riding a mule. It turned out to be the steward of the blood from the *Kulla* of Orosh, travelling God knows where. Having gone a little farther, Gjorg turned his head, as if to make sure that it was the steward of the blood. The other man had also turned around to look at him. "What's the matter with him?" Gjorg thought.

Once someone told him that he had seen a carriage that was just like Gjorg's description, but it was empty. Another time, someone described the carriage's appearance with great accuracy, and even the head of the beautiful traveller, whose hair, through the window, had seemed auburn to some people and nut-brown to others.

At least she's still here, on the High Plateau, he thought. At least she hasn't yet gone down to the plain.

Meanwhile, the month of April was wearing on swiftly. The days went on, one after the other, without a pause, and the month that even without the coming end of his truce seemed to him the shortest of the year, was getting shorter, wearing itself out swiftly.

He did not know in what direction he ought to travel. Sometimes he wasted time on the wrong road, and sometimes he went back, not by design, to a place where he had already been. His suspicion that he was not going in the right direction tormented him more and more. At last he had the conviction that he would never go anywhere but in the wrong direction, to the very end of the handful of days that was left to him, unhappy moonstruck pilgrim, whose April was to be cut off short.

CHAPTER VI

The Vorpsis went on with their trip. Bessian looked at his wife from the side. Her features were somewhat drawn, and she was a little pale, which made her look only the more desirable, as had happened a few days ago. She is tired out, he thought, even though she won't admit it. Actually, during all those days he had been waiting to hear her say at last the words that would have been so natural, "Oh, I'm so tired." He had waited for those words impatiently, feverishly, the remedy for their trouble, but she had not said them. Her face pale, she looked out at the road in silence, or very nearly. As for her expression, which even when she was angry or humiliated had always seemed understandable to him, he now found that he had no clue to what it might mean. If only her eyes expressed annoyance, or worse, coldness. But there was something else in her eyes. In some way her look was empty at its center and only the edges were still there.

Seated side by side, they rarely spoke. Sometimes he tried to create a bit of warmth, but fearing that he might put himself in a position of inferiority, he did that with great discretion. The worst of it was that he felt quite unable to be angry at her. In his relations with women he had noticed that anger and quarrelling could at times bring about a sudden resolution of static situations that had seemed hopeless, as a storm can clear away an oppressively humid atmosphere. But there was something in the way that her eyes were set that defended her against anyone else's anger. Something like the eyes of pregnant women. At one moment he even wondered—almost aloud—can she be expecting a child? But his mind, mechanically, reckoned up the time that had passed, and this disposed of his last hope. Bessian suppressed a sigh that he did not want her to hear, and he went on looking at the country-side. Night was falling.

For a little while that mood stayed with him, and when he began to think actively again, his mind brought him back to the same place. If only she would tell him that she had no heart for this trip, that she felt terribly disappoint-ed, that his notion to spend their honeymoon on the High Plateau had proved to be idiotic, that they would do well to go back at once, this very day, this instant. But when he made a vague allusion to their leaving early, so as to give her a chance to express that wish, she said, "As you like. But in any case, please don't feel troubled on my account."

Of course the idea of breaking off their trip and going home tormented him more and more, but he entertained a vague hope that something might still be saved. Indeed, he felt that if something were to be saved, that could only happen while they were on the High Plateau, and that once they went down there would be no chance of a remedy.

Now it was full night and he could not see her face. Two or three times he leaned towards the window, but he could not tell where they were. A little later the moon shed its light on the road and he put his head close to the glass. He stayed a long while in that position, and the vibration of the cold pane entered his forehead and went all through his body. In the moonlight the road looked like glass to him. The silhouette of a small church slid off to his left. Then a water-mill loomed up, and one might think that in this waste it had been built to grind snow rather than corn. His hand sought his wife's hand on the seat.

"Diana," he said softly, "look out there. I think this is a road protected by the *bessa*."

She put her face to the windowpane. Still speaking softly, using few words, and imposing upon them an order that seemed to him less and less natural, he explained to her what a road protected by the *bessa* was. He felt that the icy moonlight helped him with his task.

Then, when his words were spent, he moved his head towards her neck and kissed her timidly. The moonlight grazed her knees a number of times. She did not move, she came no closer nor did she draw away from him. Her body gave off still the odor of the perfume that he loved, and with an effort he repressed a groan. His last hope was that something would let go inside her. He hoped to hear a sob from her, if only a faint one, or at least a sigh. But she did not relinquish her strange attitude, silent but not completely, desolate as a field strewn with stars might be desolate. "O Lord," he said to himself, "what is happening to me?"

The sky was only partly overcast. The horses trotted

169

lightly on the ill-paved road. It was the Road of the Cross. From behind the glass, Bessian looked out on a landscape grown familiar to him. Except that this time, here and there, in places close to him and far away, it lay under a bluish coverlet. The snow had begun to melt, it wore away from the bottom up, from its contact with the soil, leaving above the hollow thus formed a kind of crust that scarcely melted at all.

"What day is it?" Diana asked.

Surprised, he looked at her for a moment before he replied.

"The eleventh."

She seemed about to say something. Speak to me, he thought. Please speak. Hope invaded him like a hot vapor. Say anything, but speak to me.

Her lips that he was watching out of the corner of his eye moved again to say in a different way perhaps the words she had not spoken.

"Do you remember that mountaineer we saw the day that we were on our way to the prince?"

"Yes," he said, "of course."

What did that "of course" mean, spoken so naturally? For a moment he pitied himself, without knowing why. Perhaps because he had been so eager to keep this exchange going at any cost. Perhaps, too, for a different reason that he could not specify just then.

"The truce he had been granted was to end around mid-April, wasn't it?"

"Yes," he said, "something like that. Yes, that's right, just in mid-April."

"I don't know why that came to mind," she said, still looking out of the window. "It just came, for no good reason."

"For no good reason," he repeated. Those words seemed to him to be dangerous as a ring with poison in it. Somewhere inside him a knot of rage was forming. So you did all that for no good reason? For nothing, just to torture me? But the wave of anger toppled and broke at once.

Two or three times in these last days she had turned her head to look at the young mountaineers that they passed on the road. He understood that she thought she had recognized the young man who had been at the inn, but he attached no importance to that. And now that she had mentioned him, he still felt that way.

The carriage stopped suddenly, interrupting his train of thought.

"What is it?" he said, to no one in particular.

The coachman, who had climbed down from the box, appeared a moment later near the window. His arm extended, he was pointing at the road. Only then did Bessian see an old mountain woman squatting by the roadside. She was looking at them, and she seemed to be muttering something. Bessian opened the carriage door.

"There's an old woman over there by the roadside. She says that she can't move," the coachman said.

Bessian stepped down from the carriage, and after taking a few steps for the sake of his stiff legs, he went over to the old woman, who now and again was crying out softly while clasping her knee with her hands.

"What's the matter, good mother?" Bessian asked.

"Oh, it's this accursed cramp," the old woman said. "I've been rooted here since morning, my child."

Like all the mountain women of that district, she wore a cloth dress decorated with embroidery, and a scarf on her head that showed a few wisps of grey hair.

"I have been waiting since morning for one of God's

171

creatures who could help me away from here."

"Where are you from?" the coachman asked her.

"From the village over there." The woman stretched out her arm, pointing uncertainly. "It's not far, just along the highway."

"Let's take her with us," Bessian said.

"Thank you, my son."

With the coachman's help, he lifted her up carefully, supporting her under her arms, and the two men led her to the carriage. Diana watched from inside the vehicle.

"Good day, daughter," the old woman said when she was in the carriage.

"Good day, good mother," Diana said, moving in order to give her room.

"Ah," the old woman said as the carriage moved off, "I spent the whole morning all alone by the roadside. There wasn't a living soul to be seen anywhere. I thought I was going to die there."

"It's true," Bessian said, "this road is almost deserted. Your village is a big one, isn't it?"

"Yes, it's big," the woman said, her face darkening, "It's big all right, I should say so, but what good is that?"

Bessian was looking attentively at the old woman's features and their somber expression. For a moment he thought he detected signs of hostility towards the people of her village, because no one had come by to help her and everyone had forgotten her. But the emotion that had clouded her face was something much deeper than momentary annoyance.

"Yes, my village is quite big, but most of the men are cloistered in the towers. That's why I was all alone, abandoned on the road, and almost died there."

"Cloistered because of blood-vengeance?"

"Yes, my son, for blood-vengeance. Nobody has ever seen anything to match it. Well, of course people have killed one another within the village, but never anything like this."

The old woman took a deep breath.

"Of the two hundred households of our village, only twenty are not involved in the blood-feud."

"How can that possibly be?"

"You'll see for yourself, my boy. The village looks as if everything had turned to stone, as if the plague had struck it."

Bessian put his head near the window, but the village was not yet in sight.

"Two months ago," the mountain woman said, "I myself buried a nephew, a boy beautiful as an angel."

She began to talk about that boy, and to tell how he had been killed, but as she spoke—and this was strange—the order of the words in her sentences began to change. And not only their order but the spaces between them, as if a special atmosphere was clothing them, painful and disturbing. As happens with fruit before it is fully ripe, her language changed from its ordinary condition to quite another condition, the prelude to song or lamentation. It would seem that this is how the songs of the bards come about, Bessian thought.

He was looking fixedly at the old mountain woman. That state of feeling that preceded song was accompanied by corresponding changes in the expression of her face. In her eyes there was lamentation, but no tears. And they seemed all the more disconsolate.

The carriage entered the village, followed by the echo-

173

ing clatter of its wheels on the empty road. On either side stone *kullas* rose up, seeming even more silent in broad daylight.

"This *kulla* belongs to the Shkreli, and that one, farther along, to the Krasniq, and the blood-vengeance that must be carried out is so mixed up that no one really knows which clan is the one that is supposed to take vengeance now, so much so that both families are holed up in their towers. That tower over there, the one that is three storeys high, belongs to the Vithdreq, who are feuding with the Bunga, whose *kulla* you can hardly see from here—the one whose walls are made partly of black stone. And those are the towers of the Karakaj and the Dodanaj, who are feuding, and each of those families has carried out two coffins through their doors this spring. As for those other *kullas* over that way, in the same line and facing each other, they belong to the Ukas and the Kryezeze, but since they are within rifle-shot, not just the men of each house but even the women and the young girls open fire on one another from inside their walls and do not go out."

The mountain woman went on talking in this way while the two outlanders turned to this window and that in an attempt to grasp the meaning of this strange form of civic life governed by the blood-feud as she described it to them. There was no sign of life in the heavy silence of those *kullas*. The pallid sunlight falling obliquely on their stonework only emphasized their desolate air.

They set down the old woman not far from the center of the village, and they accompanied her to her own *kulla*. Then the carriage started off again through that stone kingdom, that looked as if it were under a spell. And just imagine that there are people behind those walls and their narrow loopholes, Bessian thought. There are ardent

174

young women and young wives. And for a moment it seemed to him that despite that stiff carapace he could feel the pulsing of life, fearfully intense and beating against the walls with Beethovian power. The outside, however, the walls, the rows of loopholes, the pallid sunlight falling upon them, gave nothing away. And suddenly he cried out to himself, what is all that to you? You'd better concern yourself with your wife's unyielding stiffness. He felt rage rising swiftly in him, and he turned to Diana to break that unbearable silence once and for all, to speak to her, to demand an explanation to the very last detail, of the mute riddle of her conduct towards him.

It was not the first time that he had been on the point of doing that. Dozens of times he had rehearsed what he would say, from the most gentle appeal, Diana, what's the matter? Tell me what's troubling you, to the harshest reproofs, of the kind one can't compose without the word "devil"—what the devil is wrong with you? What the devil do you mean by that? Oh, go to the devil! In these cases, he found, that word was irreplaceable. And right now, in that haze of rage that was upon him, it was the first word that occurred to him, ready to be a part of any sentence whatever, glad to be of use, eager to take part in the argument. Well, just as in all those other times, not only could he not use that word against her, but like a man who has made a mistake and means to make amends and be responsible for the consequences, he used it against himself. He was still turned towards her, and instead of speaking harshly to her, he said to himself, what the devil is wrong with you?

What the devil is wrong with me? Just as on those other occasions, he avoided giving himself an answer. Later. Later, perhaps, the opportunity would present itself. He had not understood until now just why he had not de-manded an explanation. Now he felt that he did know why; it was that he was afraid of what she might answer. It was a fear akin to what he had experienced one winter night in Tirana in the course of a spiritualist seance at a friend's house, when they were preparing themselves to hear the voice of one of their group who had died some time ago. Bessian did not quite know why, but he could only imagine that Diana's explanation would be of the same kind, delivered as if from behind a curtain of smoke.

It was a long while since the carriage had left behind it that doomed village, and he told himself again that the only reason that he had put off having it out with his wife was fear. I'm afraid of what she might say, he thought, I'm afraid, but why?

The feeling that he was to blame had become even stronger during their journey. In fact that feeling had arisen much earlier, and perhaps he had undertaken this tour in order to rid himself of it. Well, the contrary effect had manifested itself. And now, apparently, the possibility that Diana's response might have some connection with that feeling of culpability on his part was enough to make him tremble inwardly. No, it would be better that she keep silent all through this dreadful trial, that she turn into a mummy, and that he never hear her say to him the things that would give him pain.

At some places the road was full of holes, and the carriage lurched violently. As they were going by some pools of water formed by the melting snow, she asked him, "Where are we going to have lunch?"

He turned his head, astonished. Those simple words gave him a warm feeling.

"Wherever we can," he said. "Do you have an idea?"

"No, no, that's fine," she said.

He was about to turn his whole body towards her, but he felt a strange misgiving, as if he had beside him a fragile glass object that kept him motionless.

"We might even stay the night in some inn," he said, without turning his head.

"If you wish."

He felt a wave of warmth flooding his chest. Couldn't all this be quite simple, and he, with his habit of complicating things, had he not seen the beginning of a tragedy where perhaps there was only the fatigue of the trip, an ordinary headache, or something of that sort?

"In some inn," he said, "the first one we come to."

She consented with a nod.

Perhaps it will be really much better that way, he thought happily. They had been spending their nights in the houses of strangers, with friends of friends, or more accurately, with the links of a chain of friends who had a single origin: the person with whom they had spent the first night of their journey, the only person they had known before. And every night there was a repetition of more or less the same scene—words of welcome, conversation in the living room around the fireplace, topics such as the weather, cattle, the government. Then dinner, accompanied by the most carefully considered phrases, then coffee, and the next morning, their departure, attended by the traditional escort who accompanied them to the borders of the village. In sum, all that could get to be pretty tiresome for a young bride.

"An inn!" he cried out in his thoughts. An ordinary inn beside the road, that was where salvation lay. Why hadn't he thought of it earlier? How stupid I am, he told himself happily. An inn, even a dirty one that smelled of cattle, would bring them closer together by surrounding them, if not with the kind of comfort it could not possibly provide, then with its dire poverty in whose depths there gleamed ten times more bright the happiness of temporary guests.

An inn loomed up beside the road sooner than they had expected. It rose in the midst of a barren stretch of land at the crossing of the Road of the Cross and the Great Road of the Banners, where there was no village to be seen nor any other sign of life.

"Do you serve meals?" Bessian asked as soon as he had passed the threshold.

The innkeeper, a tall, ungainly fellow with half-closed eyes answered between clenched teeth, "Cold beans."

On seeing Diana and the coachman, who was carrying a travelling bag, the innkeeper became somewhat more lively, and he grew quite attentive when he heard one of the carriage horses neighing. He rubbed his eyes and said in a hoarse voice, "Welcome, ladies and gentlemen! We can give you fried eggs and cheese. I have raki* too."

They sat down at the end of a long oak table that, as in most of the inns, took up the greater part of the common room. Two mountaineers, seated on the floor in one corner, looked curiously in their direction. A young woman was sleeping, her head resting on her baby's cradle. Close by her, on a heap of many-colored bags, someone had set down a *lahoute*.

While waiting for the innkeeper to bring them their meal, they looked about them in silence.

"The other inns were more lively," Diana said at last. "This one is very quiet."

---

* A colorless kind of spirits flavored with aniseed, distilled and drunk under many names in the Mediterranean and the Middle East.

"Better that way, don't you think?" Bessian looked at his watch. "Though at this time of day. . . . " His thoughts were elsewhere and his fingers kept up a drumming on the table. "But it doesn't look too bad here, does it?"

"That's true, especially from outside."

"It has a steep roof, the kind you like."

She nodded. Despite her weariness, her expression was softer.

"Shall we sleep here tonight?"

As he said the words, Bessian felt his heart pounding, as if in secret. What is happening to me? he said to himself.

When she was still unmarried and she had come to his place for the first time, he had been less stirred than he was now, when she was his wife. It's enough to drive you crazy, he thought.

"If you like," she said.

"What's that?"

She looked at him in surprise.

"You asked me if I would like it if we slept here tonight, didn't you?"

"And you would?"

"Yes, of course."

That's marvellous, he thought. He wanted to kiss that much-loved head that had been torturing him all these past days. A wave of warmth, of a kind he had never felt before, flooded through him. After so many nights of being separated, they would sleep together at last, in this isolated mountain inn, among these desolate roads. It was lucky, really, that things had happened this way. If not for that, he would never have known the sensation that few men have had occasion to experience—to re-live one's first embrace of a loved woman. She had become so distant in

179

these days that now he felt that he was rediscovering her as she had been when he had known her before they were married. More, this second discovery seemed to him even sweeter and more unsettling. People are right to say it's an ill wind that blows no one any good.

He sensed something moving behind him, and all at once, right under his eyes, as if coming at him from the world of the commonplace, were certain circular objects that gave off a piquant smell and were quite useless: the plates of fried eggs.

Bessian looked up.

"Do you have a good room for tonight?"

"Yes, sir," the innkeeper said confidently. "One with a fireplace at that."

"Really? That's splendid."

"Oh, yes," the innkeeper went on. "There's no room like it in all the inns of the district."

I'm really in luck, Bessian thought.

"I'll take you to it as soon as you've had your lunch," the innkeeper said.

"Splendid."

He had no appetite. Diana did not eat her eggs, either. She asked for some cream cheese, but she left it in the dish because it was dry and hard. Then she asked for yoghurt, and at last for eggs again, but boiled this time. Bessian ordered the same thing, but he ate nothing.

Right after lunch, they went upstairs to see the room. The chamber that, according to the innkeeper, was the envy of all the inns in that district of the High Plateau, was the plainest imaginable, with two windows, both with wooden shutters, facing north, and a large bed covered by a thick woolen counterpane. It did indeed have a fireplace, and there were ashes on the hearth.

"It's a fine room," Bessian said, looking questioningly at his wife.

"And can one have a fire?" she asked the landlord.

"Certainly. Right away if you wish."

For the first time in a long while, Bessian thought he saw a gleam of pleasure in Diana's eyes.

The innkeeper went away, and came back with an arm-load of wood. He lit the fire in a clumsy manner that showed it was something that he did very rarely. Both of them looked on as if it were the first time in their lives that they were looking at a fire kindled in a fireplace. He left at last, and Bessian, alone with his wife, felt again the secret pounding within his chest. Several times his eyes slid over to the large bed, with its counterpane the color of milk, which made it look warm. Diana was standing by the fire, her back turned to her husband. Timidly, as if he were drawing near to a stranger, Bessian took two steps towards her and put his arms around her shoulders. Her arms crossed, she did not move while he began to kiss her neck and then to kiss her near her lips. At times, from the side, he caught a glimpse of the red glow of the flame reflected on her cheek. Then, as his caresses grew more pressing, she said gently, "No, not now."

"Why not?"

"It's too cold. Besides, I have to have a bath."

"You're right," he said, planting a kiss on her hair. Without saying anything more, he moved away from her and left the room. The lively sound of his footfalls on the stairs showed his pleasant mood. He came a few moments later, carrying a large iron bucket full of water.

"Thank you," Diana said with a smile.

As if he were drunk, he set down the bucket on the fire, and then, looking as if he were thinking of something quite definite, he bent down to look under the mantel-piece, repeated that several times while keeping the sparks away with his hands, and found what he had been looking for, it seemed, since he called out, "There it is."

Diana too, bent down, and she saw the end of a pot-hook black with soot, hanging above the fire as in most of the fireplaces of the countryfolk. Bessian picked up the bucket, and supporting himself with one hand on the masonry of the fireplace, tried to hang it on a notch of the pot-hook.

"Careful," Diana said, "you'll burn yourself."

But the bucket was already in place, and Bessian was blowing gaily on his slightly reddened hand.

"Did you burn yourself?"

"Oh, it's nothing."

Someone was coming up the stairs. It was the coach-man, bringing them their bags. Watching him with an abstracted smile, Bessian was thinking that those people who were coming and going on the stairs, bringing wood or their luggage, were arranging things so that he might be happy. He could scarcely keep still.

"What if we go downstairs for coffee until our room and the water are warmed up?"

"Coffee? If you like. But maybe it would be better to take a walk. I'm still a little dazed with travelling."

A moment later they went down the stairs, that creaked under their tread, and Bessian told the innkeeper to take care of the fire because they were going to take a walk.

"Can you tell me if there's a picturesque spot in the neighborhood, some place really worth seeing?"

"Something worth seeing in the neighborhood?" He shook his head. "No, sir. These parts are pretty much a desert."

"Really?"

"Yes, except. . . . Wait a bit. You have a carriage, don't you? That makes a difference. A half-hour, three quarters of an hour at most if your horses aren't tired, you can get to Upper White Water to see the Alpine lakes."

"Upper White Water is only a half-hour ride by carriage?" Bessian asked in surprise.

"Yes, sir. A half-hour, or three-quarters of an hour at most. Foreign visitors who come by this way never miss the opportunity to go there."

"What do you think," Bessian said, turning to his wife. "It's true that we are tired of riding in the coach, but still it's really worth seeing that village. Particularly for the famous lakes."

"We learned that in geography class," she said.

"The air is wonderful up there. And then, all the while our room will be warming up. . . . " He broke off to look meaningfully at her.

"Fine, let's go," she said.

The innkeeper went out to call the coachman, who came in a few moments later, looking not too pleased. He had to harness the horses once more, but he was careful not to say anything against it. Climbing into the carriage, Bessian told the innkeeper yet another time to see to the fire. At the last minute, he wondered, just for an instant, if he had not been wrong in leaving behind so easily the room at the inn that he had been at pains to secure, but he was reassured at once by the thought that after a pleasant tour, Diana would be feeling better in every respect.

The afternoon sun shone gently on the moorland. A crimson tint, with no apparent source, put a touch of warmth into the air.

"The days are getting longer," Bessian said, and he

thought, Don't I find the most interesting things to say! The weather is still fine. The days are getting longer.

These were things that people who have nothing to say to each other cling to in order to fill the emptiness of their conversations. Had they become strangers to each other so that they must have recourse to phrases of that sort? That's enough, he thought, as if dismissing something regrettable. It's already done.

A half-hour later, Upper White Water did in fact come in sight. In the distance, the towers looked as if they were covered with moss. In places the snow had not yet melted, the patches of bare earth looked all the darker.

The carriage followed the road towards the lakes, along the edge of the village. As they stepped down, they heard the bells of a church ringing. Diana was the first to stop. She turned in order to find where the sounds were coming from, but she did not see the belfry. All she could see were the patches of black earth alternating bleakly with the sheets of snow. She turned away from them, and leaned on her husband's arm. They were walking towards one of the lakes.

"How many are there?" Diana asked.

"Six, I think."

They walked side by side on the thick dark brown carpet formed by successive layers of dead leaves, here and there richly rotten, as if suffering a luxurious disease. Bessian felt that his wife was getting ready to say something to him. She appeared uneasy, but the sound of the leaves underfoot seemed to relieve her in part.

"There's another lake," she said suddenly, on seeing the shoreline through the fir trees, and when he turned his head in that direction, she went on: "Bessian, surely you'll write something better about these mountains." He turned as if something had stung him in the back. He almost said, "What?", but at the last instant he stifled that exclamation. It would be better not to hear that suggestion again. He felt that someone had pressed a white-hot horseshoe to his forehead.

"After this trip," she said gently, "it would be natural if . . . . something truer. . . . "

"Yes, of course, of course."

The glowing horseshoe was still pressed against his forehead. Part of the mystery was dispelled. The mystery of her silence. In fact it had never been that. He had been waiting, almost as a certainty, for her to say those words before the first night of their new love, as the price of their understanding, of their pact.

"I understand, Diana," he said in a voice that was strangely weary. "Of course, it's hard for me, but I understand—"

She interrupted him. "This is really a wonderful place. How right we were to come here."

Bessian walked on, his thoughts elsewhere, and so they came to the second lake, and then they began to retrace their steps. On the way he got hold of himself; he was thinking of the room with the fireplace that was waiting for them, all warm, at the inn.

They came to the place where they had left their carriage, but instead of getting in they turned towards the village. The coach followed them.

The first persons they met on the way, two women carrying casks of water on their heads, slowed their steps and looked at them for a moment. In contrast, with the beauty of the countryside, the towers, close up, seemed especially gloomy. The village streets and especially the little square in front of the church were filled with people.

185

Those tight trousers of heavy wool, milk-colored, with its black stripe, oddly like the symbol of an electrical discharge, that ran down their sides, expressed all the agitation that marked their bearing.

"Something must have happened," Bessian said.

They watched the people for a moment, trying to imagine what might have occurred. But, apparently, what had happened must have been something rather peaceful and solemn.

"Is that tower the one that is the tower of refuge?" Diana asked.

"Probably. It looks like one."

Diana slowed her step to look at the tower rising somewhat apart from the others.

"If the truce that was granted to that mountaineer we saw—you know, the one we talked about today—if the truce ended in the last few days, he would certainly have taken refuge in a tower of that sort, wouldn't he?"

"Oh, certainly," Bessian said, still looking at the crowd.

"And if, at the expiration of the truce, the murderer is on the highway, far from his own village, he could take shelter in any one of those towers of refuge?"

"I think so. It's the same as with travellers overtaken by night who go into the first inn they find on the road."

"So that he could very well have sought refuge in this very tower?"

Bessian smiled.

"It's possible. But I don't think so. There are many towers, and besides, we met that man a long way from here."

Diana turned her head once more towards the *kulla*, and, in the depths of her stare and the corners of her eyes,

Bessian thought he detected something like a gentle yearning. But in that instant he saw in the crowd someone who was waving at him. A checkered vest, some familiar faces.

"Take a look at who's over there," Bessian said, with a gesture of his head in their direction.

"Well, Ali Binak," Diana said in a low voice that expressed neither satisfaction nor annoyance.

They met in the center of the square. The surveyor seemed to have drunk one glass too many this time, too. The doctor's pale eyes, and not his eyes alone but all of the delicate skin of his face, were sorrowful. As for Ali Binak, one could just make out, behind his customary coldness, a mournful weariness. The group of experts was attended by a small knot of mountaineers.

"You are going on with your journey through the High Plateau?" Ali Binak asked them in his sonorous voice.

"Yes," Bessian said. "We shall be in this district a few days more."

"The days are getting longer now."

"Yes, we're in the middle of April. And you, what are you doing in these parts?"

"What are we doing here?" the surveyor said. "As usual, running from one village to another, from one Banner to another. Portrait of a group with bloodstains. . . . "

"What?"

"Oh, I just wanted to use an image—how shall I say—well, borrowed from painting."

Ali Binak darted a cold glance at the speaker.

"Is there some dispute here that you must arbitrate?" Bessian asked Ali Binak.

The latter nodded.

"And what a dispute!" the surveyor interposed again.

"Today," he said, with a jerk of the hand to indicate Ali Binak, "he has pronounced judgment in a way that will go down in history."

"One mustn't exaggerate," Ali Binak said.

"It's no exaggeration," the surveyor said. "And this gentleman is a writer and we really must describe to him the case that you settled."

In a few minutes the case for which Ali Binak and his assistants had been called to the village had been related by several speakers at once, particularly the surveyor, and they interrupted, amplified, or corrected one another. Things appeared to have happened in this fashion:

A week ago the members of a certain family had put to death one of their girls, who was pregnant. There was no doubt that they would promptly kill as well the boy who had seduced her. In the meantime, the boy's family learned that the baby whom the young woman had not been able to bring into the world was a male child. The family forestalled their adversaries by declaring that they were the injured party in regard to the young woman's kin, and argued that while the young man was not connected with the victim by marriage, the male child belonged to him. In so doing, the boy's family made the claim that they were the ones who had a transgression to avenge, and that accordingly, it was their turn to kill a member of the young woman's family. In that way, they not only protected their guilty boy against the punishment that awaited him, but also, by tying the hands of the adverse party, prolonged the de facto peace at their convenience. It goes without saying that the other family vigorously contested this view of the case. The business was brought before the village council of elders, who found it very hard to resolve. The parents of the young woman, devastated by their misfortune, were understandably outraged by the notion that they owed a victim to their adversaries when it was precisely a boy of that house who had brought about the death of their daughter. They insisted that another solution had to be found. And what further complicated the situation was that, according to the *Kanun*, a male child from the moment of conception belonged to the family of the boy, and must be avenged on the same principle as one avenges a man. The council of elders, declaring themselves unable to pronounce on the question, appealed to the great expert on the *Kanun*, Ali Binak.

The case had been considered an hour ago (just when we were walking on the banks of the lakes, Bessian thought). The judgment, as in all matters arising from the *Kanun*, was rendered promptly. The spokesman for the boy's family had said to Ali Binak, "I should like to know why they spilled out my flour [meaning the baby that had been conceived]." And Ali Binak answered him at once: "What was your flour looking for in someone else's flour sack [meaning the womb of the young stranger woman, not bound properly by marriage]." Both parties were thus non-suited, and both were declared blameless and not bound to seek vengeance.

Impassive, with never the quiver of a muscle in his pale face, not speaking at all, Ali Binak listened to the noisy account of how he had pronounced judgment.

"There's nothing for it—you're a wonder," the surveyor said, his eyes wet with drunkenness and admiration.

They began to walk aimlessly around the square.

"When all is said and done, if you think about it calmly, these are really simple matters," said the doctor, who was walking along with Bessian and Diana. "Even this last case, which seems so dramatic, is really a question of the relation of creditor to debtor."

He went on talking, but Bessian was scarcely paying attention. He had another concern. Didn't a discussion of this kind tend to have a bad effect on Diana? During the last two days they had rather neglected matters like these, and her face had begun at last to look less troubled.

"And what about you? How did you happen to settle on the High Plateau?" Bessian said in order to change the subject. "You're a doctor, aren't you?"

The doctor said, with a bitter smile, "I was one. Now I'm something else."

His eyes showed his deep distress, and Bessian thought that light-colored eyes, even the ones that seem at first sight almost colorless, can reflect an inner pain more fully than any other kinds of eyes.

"I studied surgery in Austria," he said. "I was among the first and only group of scholarship students that was sent there by the monarchy. Perhaps you have heard what became of most of those students when they returned from foreign parts. Well, I'm one of those. Absolute disappointment, no clinical practice, no possibility of working in my profession. I was unemployed for some time, and then, just by chance, in a café in Tirana, I met that man—" and he motioned with his head towards the surveyor— "who suggested I take up this peculiar trade."

"Portrait of a group with bloodstains," said the surveyor, who had just come up to them and was following their conversation. "You'll always find us wherever there is blood."

190

The doctor ignored those words.

"And is it as a doctor that you assist Ali Binak in his work?" Bessian asked.

"Of course. Otherwise he would not take me with him."

Bessian looked at him in surprise.

"There's nothing to be surprised at there. In judgments made in accordance with the Code, particularly when it is a question of blood-letting, and most of all in the matter of wounds, the presence of someone with an elementary knowledge of medicine is always necessary. Naturally, there is no need for a surgeon's services. I would even say that the irony of my situation is precisely that I perform work that can be done quite well by the most junior kind of nurse, not to say anyone at all who has a rudimentary knowledge of the anatomy of the human body."

"Rudimentary knowledge? Is that enough?"

The doctor smiled the same bitter smile.

"The trouble is that you are sure that my function here is to dress and cure wounds—isn't that so?"

"Yes, of course. I can understand that, for the reasons you've mentioned, you gave up your profession as a surgeon—but you can still treat wounds, can't you?"

"No," the doctor said. "There would be some compensation in that. But I have nothing to do with things of that kind. Do you understand? Nothing at all. The mountaineers have always treated their wounds themselves, and they are still doing that to this very day, with raki, tobacco, in accordance with the most barbaric practices, as, for example, dislodging a bullet with another bullet, etc. So they will never call on a doctor for his services. And I am

191

here to fulfill a very different function. Do you understand? I am not here as a doctor but as the assistant to a judge. Does that seem odd to you?"

"Not entirely," Bessian said. "I have some knowledge of the *Kanun* myself, and I can imagine what you are dealing with."

"I count the wounds, classify them, and do nothing else."

For the first time Bessian had the feeling that the doctor was getting irritated. He turned to Diana, but their eyes did not meet. There was no question that this discussion would not make a good impression on her, but he told himself, too bad; provided that this comes to a stop as soon as possible, and we can get away from here.

"Perhaps you know that, according to the *Kanun*, the wounds inflicted are paid for by fines. Each wound is paid for individually, and the price depends on the part of the body in which the wound is situated. The compensation for head wounds, for example, is twice as high as that for wounds on the trunk, the latter being divided into two further categories, according to whether they are about or below the waist, and there are further distinctions. My work as an assistant consists of this only—to determine the number of the wounds and where they occur."

He looked at Bessian and then at his wife, as if he wanted to be sure of the effect of his words.

"Wounds present problems when it comes to rendering judgment—rather more problems than outright killing. You must know that by the terms of the *Kanun*, a wound that has not been compensated for by the payment of a fine is regarded as the equivalent of half of a man's blood. A wounded man, accordingly, is considered to be half-dead, a kind of shadow. In short, if someone wounds two persons in a family, or the same person twice, he becomes, by virtue of that fact—if he has not paid compensation for each of the two wounds considered separately—a debtor to the extent of all of one man's blood, which is to say a human life."

The doctor fell silent for a moment to give them time to absorb the meaning of his words.

"All that," he went on, "gives rise to extremely complicated problems, principally economic ones. You are looking at me as if you are surprised, aren't you? There are families that are unable to pay the compensation for two wounds, and they choose to discharge the debt by taking a human life. There are others that are ready to ruin themselves, to pay for as many as twenty wounds received by the victim, in order to keep the right, once their victim is well again, to murder him. Strange, isn't it? But here's something that puts all that in the shade. I know a man from the Black Ravines, who has supported his family for years on the indemnities he has received for the wounds his enemies have inflicted. He has escaped death several times, and he is convinced that, thanks to the training that he has had, he can escape dying by any bullet whatsoever, and without a doubt he is the first man in the world to create in some sense this new trade—that of making a living from his wounds."

"Horrible," Bessian muttered. He looked at Diana, and she seemed to him to be even more pale. This conversation must stop as soon as possible, he thought. Now the room at the inn, the fireplace, and the kettle of hot water hanging on the crane seemed far away. Let's get away from here, he said to himself again. Let's get away right now.

The people in the square had broken up into small groups, and Diana and Bessian were alone with the doctor.

"Perhaps you know," the doctor went on—and Bessian was on the point of interrupting him and saying, I don't know and I don't want to know—"that according to the *Kanun*, when two men fire at each other point-blank and one of them dies while the other is merely wounded, the wounded man pays the difference, as it were for the surplus blood. In other words, as I told you right at the beginning, often, behind the semi-mythical décor, you have to look for the economic component. Perhaps you'll accuse me of being cynical, but in our time, as with everything else, blood has been transformed into merchandise."

"Oh, no," Bessian said. "That's a somewhat simplistic way of looking at things. Of course economics plays a part in many things, but it won't do to go too far in that direction. And on that subject, I'd like to ask if you aren't the person who wrote an article on the blood-feud that was banned by the royal censor."

"No," the doctor said shortly. "I supplied the facts, but I was not the author."

"I think I remember reading in that article the same phraseology—blood has been turned into merchandise."

"That is an incontestable truth."

"Have you read Marx?" Bessian asked.

The doctor did not reply. He just looked at Bessian as if to say, "And you who are asking me that question, have you read him?"

Bessian glanced swiftly at Diana, who was looking straight before her, and he felt that he must argue with the doctor.

"In my opinion, even your explanation of the murder that you gave judgment on today is much too simplistic," he said, hoping to find something that he could contradict.

"Not at all. I said it and I'll repeat it. In every aspect of the events that were discussed today, it was purely a question of settling a debt."

"Yes, a debt, certainly, but a debt of blood."

"Blood, precious stones, cloth, it makes no difference. To me, it concerns a debt, and that is all."

"It's not the same thing."

"It's exactly the same thing."

The doctor's tone had become harsh. His delicate skin reddened as if it were burning. Bessian felt deeply offended.

"That is much too naive an explanation, not to say a cynical one," he said.

The doctor's eyes turned icy.

"You're the one who's naive, naive and cynical at the same time—you and your art."

"You needn't raise your voice," said Bessian.

"I'll yell my head off if I please," the doctor said, though he lowered his voice at the same time. But, coming through his lips as if he were whistling, his voice sounded all the more threatening. "Your books, your art, they all smell of murder. Instead of doing something for these unfortunate mountaineers, you help death, you look for exalted themes, you look here for beauty so as to feed your art. You don't see that this is beauty that kills, as a young writer said whom you certainly do not care for. You remind me of those theaters built in the palaces of Russian aristocrats, where the stage is large enough to accommodate hundreds of actors, while the living room can scarcely accommodate the prince's family. That's it. What you remind me of is those aristocrats. You encourage a whole nation to perform in a bloody drama, while you yourselves and your ladies watch the spectacle from your loges."

At that moment Bessian noticed Diana's absence. She had to be somewhere ahead of him, perhaps with the surveyor who would be sticking close to her, he thought, half-dazed.

"But you," he said, "I mean you personally, you who are a doctor, who claim to understand things in the right way, why do you take part in this hoax? How about it? Why do you take advantage of that situation to earn your living?"

"When it comes to what I do, you're absolutely right. I'm just a failure. But at least I understand what I am, and I don't infect the world with my books."

Bessian was looking for Diana, but he did not see her. From one point of view it was just as well that she had not heard those morbid opinions. The man went on talking and Bessian tried to listen, but as he himself was about to speak, instead of answering the doctor he said, as if he were talking to himself, "Where's my wife?"

Now he was looking for her among the people who were still walking slowly to and fro in the church square.

"Diana!" he called, on the chance that she might hear him.

A number of people turned towards him.

"She may have gone into the church out of curiosity, or into a house to go to the bathroom."

"That's possible."

They kept on walking, but Bessian was uneasy. I shouldn't have left the inn, he thought.

196

"Forgive me," the doctor said in a mild tone. "Perhaps I overdid it."

"That's nothing. Where can she have gone?"

"Don't worry. She must be right in the neighborhood. Do you feel ill? You're very pale."

"No, no. I'm all right."

Bessian felt the doctor's hand take hold of his arm, and he wanted to move away, but he forgot to do it. Some children were keeping close to the nearest group of people, the one that included Ali Binak and the surveyor. Bessian felt his mouth go bitter. The lakes, he thought, for a second only. That old carpet of leaves, hopelessly rotten, covered over with that deceptive gold.

He was striding swiftly towards the group around Ali Binak. Is she drowned, he wondered while still some distance from them. But their faces were petrified. There was nothing in their expression that could give him reassurance.

"What is it?" he asked in panic, and unconsciously, perhaps because of the expression of those faces, instead of saying, "What has happened to her?" he said, "What has she done?"

The answer came with great difficulty from pitilessly clamped jaws. They had to repeat it to him several times before he could understand: Diana had gone inside the tower of refuge.

What had happened? Not at that moment, and not later, when the witnesses started to describe what they had seen (people felt immediately that it was one of those happenings that had an element of reality and at the same time an element of mist that separated it from normal life, and therefore that it was a happening that lent itself to the

197

legendary), not at that time nor afterwards, then, could anyone establish precisely how the young woman from the capital had managed to get into the tower, where no stranger had ever set foot. And what was even more unlikely than the fact that she had entered there, was that no one had noticed it, or rather that if someone remembered that she had drawn away from the group, that she had wandered in the neighborhood, no one except for some children had paid enough attention to keep their eyes upon her. And she herself, perhaps, if she were questioned about the way in which she had gone down the road that far and had succeeded at last in entering, might she have been unable to explain anything at all? To judge by the few words that she had left behind her on the High Plateau, she would have felt at that moment something like detachment from everything, a kind of loss of gravity, which had lightened for her not only the idea of entering the tower but her going itself—all the way to the gate. And then, it should not be ignored that that very circumstance might help to turn people's attention from her, and so allow her to take the fateful step. In fact, as some persons remembered thereafter, she had drawn away from the people in the square and approached the tower as lightly as a moth fluttering towards a lamp. She was flying, as it were, and carried along in that way like a leaf in the wind, she had gone inside—or rather, fallen across the threshold.

Bessian, his face ashen, understood at last what had happened. The first thing he did was to dart out to take his wife from that place, but strong hands seized both his arms.

"Let me go!" he shouted in a hoarse voice.

Their faces were aligned around his, unmoving as the

stones of a wall. Among them was the pale face of Ali Binak.

"Let me go!" he said to him, though Ali was not one of those who were restraining him.

"Calm yourself, sir," said Ali Binak. "You cannot go over there; no one can enter there, except for the priest."

"But my wife is inside there," Bessian cried. "Alone among those men."

"You are quite right. Something must be done, but you may not go there. They could fire at you, you see. They might kill you."

"Then have someone send for the priest, or for the Devil knows who, just so one can get inside."

"The priest has been notified," Ali Binak said.

"He's coming! Here he is!" several voices said.

A small group had gathered around them. Bessian recognized his coachman, who was looking at him with eyes that seemed to be popping out of their sockets, expecting an order from him. But Bessian looked away.

"Move away!" Ali Binak said in a commanding tone. Some persons took a few steps only, and then stopped.

The priest came up, out of breath. His flabby face, with its heavy pockets beneath his eyes, looked very much alarmed.

"How long has she been inside?" he asked.

Ali Binak looked around questioningly. A number of persons spoke at once. One said half an hour, another an hour, and someone else a quarter of an hour. Most of those around shrugged their shoulders.

"That's not important," Ali Binak said. "What is needed is action."

The priest and Ali Binak conferred with each other.

Bessian heard Ali Binak say, "Then I'll go with you," and he took courage from that. In the crowd you could hear the words, "The priest is going there, together with Ali Binak."

The priest walked off, followed by Ali Binak. After taking a few steps, Ali turned around and said to the crowd, "Stay where you are. They might shoot."

Bessian felt that he was still being held by his arms. What is happening to me? he groaned inwardly. It seemed to him that the whole world was empty; all that was left was two forms in motion, the priest and Ali Binak, and the tower of refuge to which they were going.

He heard voices around him, like the distant whistling of a wind that was coming from another world. "They can't shoot the priest, since he is protected by the *Kanun*, but there's nothing to stop them from killing Ali Binak." "No, I don't think they'll fire at Ali Binak either. Everyone knows who he is."

The two men were halfway along when, suddenly, Diana appeared at the gate of the tower. Bessian could never remember clearly what happened at that moment. He remembered only that he had striven with all his strength to go to her, that his arms were gripped violently, and that voices said: Wait until she has come a bit farther, and she reaches the white stones. Then, again, he saw for a fleeting moment the figure of the doctor; he made another attempt to free himself and he heard the same voices trying to calm him.

At last Diana reached the white stones, and the men who were holding Bessian let him go, although one of them said, "Don't let him go—he'll kill her." Diana's face was white as a sheet. There was no sign of terror in it, nor pain, nor shame—only a frightening absence, especially in her eyes. Anxiously, Bessian looked for a tear in her clothing, a bluish stain on her lips or her neck, but he saw nothing of that kind. Then he heaved a sigh, and perhaps he would have felt relieved if there were not that emptiness in her eyes.

In a gesture that was not violent but not gentle either, he seized his wife's arm, and walking ahead of her he drew her towards the carriage, and they got in one behind the other, without a word and without a wave to anyone.

The carriage rolled swiftly on the highroad. How long had they been travelling in this way—a minute, a century? At last Bessian turned to his wife.

"Why don't you say something? Why don't you tell me what happened?"

She sat motionless on the seat, looking straight ahead, as if she were somewhere else. Then he seized her by the elbow, violently, harshly.

"Tell me, what did you do in there?"

She did not answer, she did not try to draw away her arm that he was squeezing like a vise.

Why did you go there, he cried out within him. To see all the horror of the tragedy with your own eyes? Or to look for that mountaineer, That Gjorg. . . . Gjorg. I'll search for you in tower after tower, eh?

He repeated those questions aloud, perhaps in other words though in the same order, but there was no answer, and he was sure that all those reasons together were responsible for that action. Suddenly, he felt a weariness such as he had never known.

Outside, night was falling. The twilight, together with the fog, spread swiftly along the road. Once he thought he saw beyond the window a man riding a mule. The traveller with the wan face whom Bessian thought he recognized followed the carriage for a short time. Where is the steward of the blood going in the dark, he wondered.

And you yourself, where are you going? He asked himself that question a moment later. Alone in these alien highlands, in the dusk peopled with phantoms, where are you going?

Half an hour later, the carriage stopped in front of the inn. One behind the other, they climbed the wooden stairs and went into the room. The fire was still alight and the water-bucket, which the innkeeper had certainly filled again, was still there, black with soot. An oil lamp gave out a wavering light. Neither troubled with the fire or the bucket. Diana undressed and lay down, lying on her back, one arm drawn over her eyes to keep the lamplight from them. He stood by the window, his eyes on the window-pane, turning only momentarily to look at that fine arm with the silken strap that had slipped from her shoulder, covering the upper part of her face. What had they done to her, the half-blind Cyclops murderers in the tower? And he felt that the question might fill up all of a human life.

They stayed at the inn that night and all the next day without leaving their room. The innkeeper brought them their meals, surprised that they did not ask to have the fire lit in the fireplace.

In the morning of the following day (it was the seventeenth of April) the coachman put their bags in the carriage, and the two, having paid the innkeeper, said goodbye coldly and set out.

They were leaving the High Plateau.

CHAPTER VII

On the morning of the seventeenth of April, Gjorg was on the highroad that led to Brezftoht. Although he had been walking since dawn without a stop, he reckoned that it would take him at least another day to reach Brezftoht, while his *bessa* came to an end at noon today.

He raised his head in order to find the sun; the clouds, high in the sky, covered it over, but one could tell its position. It's near to midday, he thought, and he turned his eyes to the road again. He was still dazed by the light overhead, and the road seemed to him to be strewn with reddish glints. While walking, he thought that if his *bessa* were over in the evening, walking very swiftly he might have been able to reach home around midnight. But, like most of the truces granted, this one was over at noon. It was well understood that if the man protected by the *bessa* was killed on the very day it expired, people would look to

203

see in what direction lay the shadow of the dead man's head. If the shadow was towards the east, that meant that he had been killed after midday, when the truce was no longer in force. If, on the contrary, the shadow was towards the west, that would show that he had been killed before the truce had expired, a cowardly act.

Gjorg raised his head again. His business, on this day, was linked with the sky and the motion of the sun. Then, as before, he lowered his dazed eyes to the road, which seemed to be drowning in the light. He turned his head and saw, spread everywhere, that uninterrupted brilliance. Apparently, the black carriage that he had looked for in vain for three weeks on all the roads of the High Plateau, was not going to appear on this last morning of his life as a free man either. How many times had he thought he had seen it loom up before him—but on each occasion the carriage seemed to have disappeared into thin air. Someone had seen it on the Road of Shadow, at the Manor Houses of Shala, on the Grand Road of the Banners, but despite his efforts he had not managed to find it. As soon as he came to the place where people said they had seen it, he found that it had just departed, and when he retraced his steps so as to intercept it on the road at some crossing where it might chance to go by, it had given him the slip again, having taken another, unforeseen direction.

Momentarily, he would forget about it, but the road itself reminded him of it, even though he had lost all hope, or nearly, of finding it again. In fact, even if the carriage were to wander forever through the High Plateau, he would very soon immure himself in the tower of refuge, and it would not be possible for him to see it; and then, even if the impossible came to pass and he were to come out one day, his eyes would be so weakened that he would be able to see no more of it than a dim spot, like the bouquet of crushed roses that the sun drew today against the background of the clouds.

Gjorg dismissed its image in his mind and began to think of his family. They would be waiting for him anxiously before noon, but he could not get there in time. Towards midday he was going to have to break off his journey and hide somewhere to wait for nightfall. Now he was a man stained with blood, and he could travel only by night and never on the main roads. The *Kanun*, far from regarding that precaution as a sign of fear, held it to be a sign of prudence and courage, for not only did it preserve the life of the murderer, but also hindered his moving about too freely and driving the family of his victim wild. While feeling satisfaction that he had done his duty, the murderer must also feel a sense of guilt before the world. In any case, at noon he would have to find a hiding place to hole up in until nightfall. These last days, in the inns where he had stopped to spend the night, more than once he had had the impression that he had seen the fleeting shape of a member of the Kryeqyqe family. Perhaps it was an illusion, but perhaps he had seen aright, and someone was on his heels in order to kill him as soon as his *bessa* was over, at a time when he had not yet become fully aware of the need to protect himself.

Whatever I do, I must be careful, he thought, and for the third time he lifted his eyes towards the sky. At that very moment he thought he heard a sound in the distance. He stopped, trying to find where it came from, but he could not. He walked on, and he heard the sound again. It was a muffled rumbling that alternately swelled and sank. It must be the sound of a waterfall, he thought. And that was indeed what it was. As he came nearer, he stopped, fascinated. In all his life, he had never seen a more wonderful waterfall. It was different from all those he had ever seen. Without throwing up foam or spurting, it flowed evenly along a dark-green rock, like thick massed tresses, that reminded Gjorg of the hair of the beautiful traveller from the capital. Under the sun's rays you could easily mistake one for the other.

He stayed a while on the small wooden bridge, under which the waters that had fallen from the rock kept on flowing, but now the current was jumbled and without majesty. Gjorg's eyes were fixed on the waterfall. A week ago, in an inn where he had spent the night, he had heard someone say that there were some countries in the world that drew electric light from waterfalls. A young mountaineer told two of the guests that he had been told that by a man who had heard it from some other one, and the guests listened to him while saying over and over, "Making light out of water? You're off your rocker, friend. Water isn't petroleum, you know, to make light with. If water drowns fire, how could it kindle fire?" But the mountaineer persisted. He had heard it explained just as he had told them, he wasn't inventing anything. They made light by means of water, but not with just any old water, because water is as different as men are. You could only do that with the noble water of waterfalls. "The people who told you that one are pretty crazy, and you're crazier still for having believed them," the guests said. But that didn't keep the mountaineer from saying that if that were to happen, if that were to happen on the High Plateau, then (once again according to what the man had told him, and who had received the information from yet another source) the *Kanun* would become somewhat more gentle and the *Rrafsh* would be rinsed somewhat of the death that flowed through it, just as poisoned lands got rid of their salt when they were irrigated. "Fool, you fool," said the guests, but Gjorg himself, God knows why, believed what the unknown source had said.

With an effort he turned his back on the waterfall. The road stretched away endlessly, almost in a straight line, and at either extremity it was lightly tinted with purple.

Again, he looked up at the sky. Just a little while now and his *bessa* would be over, he himself would be leaving the time of the *Kanun*. Leaving time, he said to himself. It seemed strange that someone could leave his time. Just a little while now, he said, looking at the sky. Now the crushed roses beyond the clouds had grown a little darker. Gjorg smiled bitterly, as if to say, There's no help for it!

Meanwhile, the coach that was carrying Bessian and Diana was rolling along the Grand Road of the Banners, the longest of all those roads that furrowed the High Plateau. The peaks half-whitened by the snow receded farther and farther, and Bessian, looking at them, was thinking that at last they were leaving the kingdom of death. Out of the corner of his right eye, he could some-times catch sight of his wife's face in profile. Pale, rigid in a way that was heightened rather than lessened by the jolting of the carriage, she was frightening to him. She seemed strange to him, mad, a body that had left its soul in the high country.

What the devil was I thinking of when I decided to take her to that accursed High Plateau? he said for the hun-dredth time. She had had just one brush with the High Plateau, and that had been enough to take her away from him. It had been enough for the monstrous mechanism merely to touch her, to ravish her away, to take her captive, or at best to make her a mountain nymph.

The squeaking of the carriage wheels were appropriate music for his doubts, his conjectures, his remorse. He had put his happiness to the test, as if he had wanted to find out whether he deserved it or not. He had directed that fragile happiness from its first spring season to the gates of hell. And it had not withstood the test.

Sometimes, when he felt calmer, he told himself that no other attachment, no third person would ever be able to change in the slightest Diana's feeling for him. If that had really come about (Lord, how bitter those words were: really come about), it had nothing to do with any third person, but that something grand and terrible had intervened. Something dark, having to do with the ordeal of millions of souls during long centuries, and for that very reason seemingly irreparable. Like a butterfly touched by a black locomotive, she had been stricken by the ordeal of the High Plateau, and had been overcome.

Sometimes, calm in a way that frightened him, he thought that perhaps he had had to pay that tribute to the High Plateau. A tribute because of his writings, for the fairies and mountain nymphs that he had described in them, and for the little loge where he had watched the play in which the actors were a whole people drowned in blood.

But perhaps that punishment might have sought him out anywhere, even in Tirana, he thought consolingly. For the High Plateau sent out its waves afar, over all the country and for all time.

He turned up his coatsleeve and looked at his watch. It was noon.

Gjorg raised his head and looked for the stain that the

sun made above the expanse of cloud. It's just noon, he thought. His *bessa* was at an end.

He jumped nimbly onto the fallows that bordered the highroad. Now he had to find a safe place in which he could wait for nightfall. On both sides of the road, the country was deserted, but he could not go on walking on the highroad. That would have seemed to him to violate the *Kanun*.

Around him was a flat expanse that went on and on. In the distance were cultivated fields and some trees, but he could not see the smallest hollow nor even some brush that would give him any cover. As soon as I can find a hiding-place, I'll be safe, he thought, as if he wanted to convince himself that if he was putting himself in danger it was not because he was deliberately playing the fool, but because there was no shelter to be found.

The moor seemed to extend to the horizon. He felt a strange calm inside his head, or rather a dull emptiness. He was absolutely alone under the sky which the weight of the sun now seemed to tilt slightly to the west. Around him, the day was just the same, bathed in the same air and the same purple shining, although the truce was over and he had entered into another time. His eyes roamed coldly all around. Was that how it looked, the time beyond the *bessa*? Eternal time, that was no longer his, without days, without seasons, without years, without a future, abstract time, to which he had no attachments of any kind. Wholly alien, it would no longer give him any sign, any hint, not even about the day when he would meet his punishment, which was somewhere in front of him, at a date and place unknown, and which would come to him by a hand equally unknown.

He was deep in these thoughts when he made out in the

distance some grey buildings that he thought he recognized. Look, those are the Manors of Rreze, he said to himself when he had come up with them. From those houses up to a brook whose name he had forgotten, the road, he believed, was under the *bessa*. The roads protected by the *bessa* had no signboards, nor any special marks, but nonetheless, everyone knew them. All he need do was to ask the first person he met.

Gjorg, walking on the moor now, quickened his pace. His mind had shaken off its somnolence. He would reach the road protected by the *bessa*, and he would stroll along on it until evening without having to cower under a bush. Meanwhile. . . . who could tell, the carriage lined with velvet might come that way. Once, people had told him, it had appeared at the Manors of Shala.

Yes, yes, that's what he would do. He turned his eyes to the left, then to the right, made certain that the road like the moor was deserted, and stepping lightly, in a few moments he reached the highroad and began to walk along it. He had taken that shortcut in order to get to the road that was under the *bessa*, failing which it would have been an hour's walk to get there.

Careful, he told himself. Now the shadow cast by his head fell to the east. But the highroad was still deserted. He walked swiftly, thinking of nothing. Far ahead he saw black figures that were hardly moving. As he came nearer, he saw that they were two mountaineers and a woman riding a donkey.

"That road over there, is it under the *bessa*?" Gjorg asked.

"Oh, yes, lad," the older man replied. "For a hundred years now, the road that runs from the Manors of Rreze to the Nymph's Brook has been protected by the *bessa*."

210

"Thank you."

"Not at all, my boy," the old man said, stealing a glance at the black ribbon on Gjorg's sleeve. "A safe journey to you."

As he strode swiftly down the road, Gjorg wondered what the killers overtaken by the end of their truce, all over the High Plateau, would do without those roads that were under the *bessa*, their places of refuge, where they were sheltered from their pursuers.

The section of the road protected by the *bessa* differed not at all from the rest of the road. It was the same ancient paving, damaged in places by horses' hooves and flowing water, with the same hollows in its surface and, at the sides, the same brush. But Gjorg felt that there was something warm about the golden dust. He took a deep breath and he slowed his pace. Here is where I'll wait for nightfall, he thought. He would sit down and rest on a stone. That would be better than hiding in a thicket. Besides, the carriage might come this way. He still had a faint hope that he might see her. And his musings went further than that: he saw the carriage stop and heard the people in it say, "Oh, mountaineer, if you're tired, climb into our carriage and ride with us a ways."

Now and again, Gjorg looked up at the sky. In three hours, at most, night would fall. Mountaineers were going by, on foot or on horseback, alone or in small groups. In the distance he could see two or three motionless specks. They must surely be murderers like himself who were waiting for night in order to travel farther. They must be worried at home, he thought.

A mountaineer came along, walking slowly and driving before him an ox that was all black.

Gjorg was walking even more slowly than the mountaineer and his ox, and they came up with him.

"Good afternoon," the man said.

"Good afternoon," Gjorg said.

The man made a gesture with his head at the sky.

"Time just doesn't go by," he said.

He had a reddish mustache that seemed to light up his smile.

"Your *bessa*'s over?"

"Yes, since noon today."

"Mine was over three days ago, but I haven't managed to sell this bull yet."

Gjorg looked at him astonished.

"For two weeks I've been tramping the roads with him, and I can't manage to sell him. He's one fine animal, all my people wept when they saw him leaving, and I can't find a buyer."

Gjorg did not know what to say. He had never had anything to do with selling cattle.

"I'd like to sell him before I shut myself up in the tower," the mountaineer went on. "The family's in bad shape, friend, and if I don't sell him myself, there won't be any one at home to sell him. But I don't have much hope anymore. If I haven't been able to sell him in the two weeks when I was still free, how am I going to sell him now that I can only go about by night? Well, what do you think?"

"You're right," Gjorg said. "It won't be easy."

Looking sidelong, he watched the black ox that was chewing calmly. The words of the old ballad of the soldier dying in a far-off country came to him: "Give my love to mother and tell her to sell the black ox."

"Where are you from?" the mountaineer asked.

"From Brezftoht."

"That's not so far from here. If you step along you can be home tonight."

"And you?" Gjorg asked.

"Oh, I'm from very far from here, from the Krasniq banner."

Gjorg whistled. "Yes, that's really far. You'll certainly have sold your bull before you get home."

"I don't think so. Now the only places where I can sell him are the roads that are under the *bessa*, and they're scarce."

Gjorg nodded.

"You see, if this road that's under the *bessa* went as far as the crossing with the Grand Road of the Banners, well, I could certainly sell him. But it ends before that."

"Is the Road of the Banners nearby?"

"It's not far. That's what I call a road! What don't you see go by there!"

"It's true, you see very odd things on the roads. Once I happened to see a carriage—"

"A black carriage with a pretty woman in it," the other man interrupted.

"How do you know that?" Gjorg cried.

"I saw her yesterday at the Inn of the Cross."

"And what were they doing there?"

"What were they doing? Nothing. The carriage didn't have the horses in the shafts, and it was just in front of the inn. The coachman was drinking coffee in it."

"And she?"

The mountaineer smiled. "They were inside the inn. They had been there two days and two nights without leaving their room. That's what the innkeeper said. Old boy, that woman was as beautiful as a fairy. Her eyes pierced you through and through. I left them behind me

213

last night. They certainly must have left today."

"How do you know?"

"The innkeeper said so. They were supposed to leave the next day. The coachman told him."

Gjorg was stunned for some moments. He stared at the paved road-surface.

"And what road do you take to get there?" he asked suddenly.

The other man pointed out the direction.

"It's an hour's walk from here. This road we're on crosses the Road of the Banners. They have to pass there, if they haven't done so already. There is no other road."

Gjorg was staring in the direction that his companion had pointed to. Now the man looked at him in surprise.

"What's the matter with you, you poor fellow?" he said.

Gjorg did not answer. An hour's walk from here, he told himself. He raised his head to look for the sun's track behind the clouds. He reckoned that there were still two hours of daylight left. She had never been so near. He would be able to see his fairy.

Without further thought, without even saying goodbye to his fellow wayfarer, he went off like a madman in the direction where, according to the man with the black ox, the crossroads lay.

The Vorpsi's carriage was leaving the High Plateau behind at a good pace. The day was ending when the roads of the little town, the tops of two minarets, and the belfry of the only church appeared in the distance.

Bessian leaned towards the carriage window; the silly lanes among the buildings he filled at once in his imagination with the small city's people, employees of the subprefecture carrying documents to the justice of the peace, with shops, with sleepy offices, and with four or five telephones of ancient vintage, the only ones in town, by means of which boring talk was carried on, mostly punctuated with yawning. He thought of all that, and all at once the world that awaited him in the capital seemed terribly pale and insipid compared with the one he had just left.

Nevertheless, he thought sadly, he belonged to that pale world, and since that was the case he ought never to have gone up to the High Plateau. It had not been created for ordinary mortals but for Titanic beings.

The smoke from the little town grew in volume. Diana, her head resting on the back of the seat, was as motionless as when they had entered the carriage. Bessian felt that he was bringing home only the outward form of his wife, and that he had left the woman herself somewhere in the mountains.

Now they were driving over the naked moor where their tour had begun a month ago. He turned his head again to see the *Rrafsh,* perhaps for the last time. The mountains were receding ever more slowly, sinking back into solitude. A white, mysterious mist came down upon them, like a curtain lowered on the play just ended.

At that moment, Gjorg was walking with long strides on the Road of the Banners, that he had reached an hour ago. The air was rippled with the first shiver of dusk when he heard, off to one side, a few short words:

"Gjorg, give my greeting to Zef Krye. . . ."

His arm, in a sudden motion, tried to slip the rifle from his shoulder, but that gesture became confounded with the syllables *qyqe,* the last half of the hateful name, which

215

made its way confusedly to his consciousness. Gjorg saw the ground reel, and then rear up violently to crash against his face. He had collapsed.

For a moment the world seemed to him to have gone absolutely still; then through that deafness he heard footsteps. He felt two hands moving his body. He's turning me on my back, he thought. But at that instant, something cold, perhaps the barrel of his rifle, touched his right cheek. God, according to the rules! He tried to open his eyes, and he could not tell if they were open or not. Instead of his murderer, he saw some white patches of snow that had not yet melted, and among those patches, the black ox, which still had not been sold. This is it, he thought, and really the whole thing has been going on too long.

Again, he heard footsteps, drawing away, and a number of times he wondered, whose steps are those? He felt that they were familiar. Yes, he knew them, and the hands that had turned him on his back. They're mine! The seventeenth of March, the road, near Brezftoht. . . . He lost consciousness for a moment, then he heard the footsteps again, and again it seemed to him that they were his own, that it was himself and no one else who was running now, leaving behind, sprawled on the road, his own body that he had just struck down.

December 1978